# A DIXIE MORRIS ANIMAL ADVENTURE

## DIXIE & FLASH

### GILBERT MORRIS

**MOODY PRESS**
CHICAGO

*To Renea*
*You have been my friend*
*through trials and tribulations.*
*I'm so grateful for that and*
*thank the Lord for you.*

©1999 by
GILBERT MORRIS

All Scripture quotations, unless indicated, are taken from the *New American Standard Bible,* © 1960, 1962, 1963, 1968, 1971, 1972, 1973, 1975, 1977, and 1994 by The Lockman Foundation, La Habra, Calif. Used by permission.

ISBN: 0-8024-3372-3

1 3 5 7 9 10 8 6 4 2

*Printed in the United States of America*

# CONTENTS

# 1
# OFF TO A DIFFERENT WORLD

Dixie took two handfuls of Blizzard's fur and pressed her face against his chest. The big dog whined and tried to turn his head to lick her face. She murmured in a muffled voice, "I'm going to miss you, Blizzard—I'm going to miss you like crazy!"

The Siberian husky gave a sudden jerk, loosing Dixie's grasp. Then, before she could move, he planted his massive paws on her shoulders. Since Dixie had been squatting down, she fell over backward. Instantly he was lapping her cheeks with his rough tongue.

"He thinks you're going to take him out for another race, Dixie."

Lars Bjoren reached down and pulled his dog away, then put an arm around Dixie. "I'm going to miss you just like you'll miss him," he said. "We've had some great times together, Dixie. I don't know what I would have done without you."

During Dixie Morris's eleven years, she had had only a few partings that were more painful than this one. She hugged the blond-bearded man and fought down the temptation to begin bawling.

Then she managed a smile for Martha Harlow. Lars Bjoren had almost wrecked his life because Martha, his childhood sweetheart, had married another man. After a time, her husband had died. But when Dixie came to Alaska only three months ago, Lars was still an angry hermit.

"I'm glad Lars has you to take care of him, Martha."

Martha Harlow was a tall blonde woman with blue green eyes. She kissed Dixie and spoke loudly over the piercing sound of the jet's engine. "You take care of Clarissa now, and I'll take of Lars. Between the two of us, we'll get them raised."

Clarissa was the reason that Dixie had come from the South to Alaska in the first place. Clarissa was to be a missionary with Dixie's parents. The plan was for Dixie to spend the summer with her, and then the two would fly out to Africa together.

Now Clarissa hurried up to them, yelling, "We've got to get on the plane! They're ready for us!"

As usual at such departings, there were many hugs and promises to write. But finally Dixie and Clarissa boarded the small commuter plane. They would fly to Nome, where they would get on a jumbo jet and begin their long trip to Africa.

Dixie did not have time to be really sad. But as the flight attendant smiled at her and said, "Glad to have you aboard," Dixie Morris knew she would be lonesome for her friends in Alaska.

"Do you want to sit by the window?" Clarissa asked. Like her mother, she was blonde and had blue green eyes.

"You can have it if you want it, Clarissa."

"That's all right. There'll be plenty to see."

Dixie fastened her seat belt as Clarissa took the seat beside her. Dixie looked out the window. Those who had come to say good-bye were waving. She waved back.

The plane began to tremble. It moved slowly forward, then picked up speed, and the tires bumped roughly over the field. She felt a sudden surge of power and saw the ground fall away beneath them. Up—up—up the plane went. It wheeled to one side, and she could see Lars and Martha looking upward. They grew smaller and smaller, and when the plane leveled, she lost sight of them.

With a deep sigh, Dixie turned to Clarissa. "I'm going to miss them a lot—but not as much as you will."

The older girl gave Dixie a quick hug and a flashing smile. "Of course, we'll both miss them. Just like you'll miss your aunt and uncle and all your friends in the States. But you'll be with your mom and dad, and I'll be doing what God has called me to do, so it'll be all right."

"It feels like Mom and Dad have been gone forever, but it's actually only been a little over a year."

Dixie looked out over the white, fleecy, elephant-shaped clouds and thought about how lonely she had been when her parents had first gone to the mission field. But then she had joined Aunt Sarah and traveled with the circus, and life had brightened up. She thought of the wonderful and beautiful animals she had known at the circus—Ruth, the massive African elephant; Stripes, the Siberian tiger; Sandy, the camel; and the rest. They all floated by in her imagination, and she thought, *I'll miss every one of them, but I'll be with Mom and Dad.*

Dixie grew very tired of flying, and when they landed at Heathrow Airport in London, she was excited. "Can we see some of the sights before we leave, Clarissa?"

"That's what I've planned. We've got an extra day here, so we're going to take about a million pictures."

And take pictures they did! They took pictures of London Bridge, of Westminster Abbey, of the Tower of London. It was a different world for Dixie. She was very interested in how different the language in England was from what she was accustomed to.

"They call things by different names here, Clarissa," she said. "They call an elevator a *lift*."

"And they call the hood of a car the *bonnet*."

Dixie suddenly giggled. "That was funny at breakfast this morning, wasn't it? I felt so silly!"

Dixie had ordered toast and jelly. The waitress looked at her with amazement. "You want jelly for breakfast?" she asked.

Being assured that Dixie did, she shrugged and went away. She brought back two pieces of toast and a bowl of strawberry Jello. "I didn't know they called Jello 'jelly' here. I wonder what they call real jelly?"

"Jam, I think. But it's been fun, hasn't it?"

"Yes, it has, and we got some good pictures to show Mom and Dad."

They made one more trip that day—to Buckingham Palace. Dixie was impressed with the tall Grenadier Guards. "But they don't ever smile," she said. "Their faces look like they're frozen!"

"They're chosen partly for that ability," Clarissa said.

"I'll bet I could make them laugh."

"I'll bet you can't!"

Dixie stood in front of a guard. She began to make faces at him. But he did not move a single muscle. She said, "Let me tell you a funny story." She told her funniest joke, but still no result.

"You just have no sense of humor," she pouted.

Clarissa laughed at her. "Come on, Dixie. Your act didn't go over very well here."

Just before going back to the hotel,

they went shopping, and Dixie used most of her spending money to buy a necklace. It had a large green stone hanging from a delicate gold chain.

"Let me put it on you," Clarissa said. She fastened the necklace and then stood back and nodded with satisfaction. "That looks beautiful!"

Dixie looked at herself in the mirror. She had long blonde hair, deep blue eyes, and looked strong and healthy. She admired the necklace. "It's so pretty! I'm going to keep it always."

Clarissa smiled. "Better be careful about making statements like that. They have a way of coming back to haunt us."

Back at the hotel, Dixie stayed up to watch TV for a while. "Isn't it funny," she said, "that they don't have any commercials?"

"That's right. And in America, sometimes the commercials are the best part of television."

Later, as she lay in the silent darkness, Dixie again thought of Africa. *It used to be called the Dark Continent, and there are all kinds of animals there. I hope it's a nice house that Dad has built—but whatever kind it is, I'll like it as long as I'm with them.*

## 2

# THE DIFFERENT WORLD

The big jet tilted to one side, and Dixie saw the glittering greenish waters of the ocean beneath.

Soon the plane swung in a larger circle and leveled off, and Clarissa cried, "See, Dixie! There's Africa!"

Eagerly Dixie gazed out the window. There was the shoreline of Africa! Her heart beat a little faster as she thought, *I've wanted so long to come here and be with Mom and Dad—and now it's actually happening!*

"Fasten seat belts," Clarissa said. "The light has come on."

Dixie snapped hers and waited. The plane got lower and lower, and she heard the roaring sound as the wing flaps were lowered. Then the wheels hit the ground, and the plane shuddered.

"Hooray! We're here!" Dixie shouted. Then she looked around in embarrassment, but she saw that the other passengers were smiling at her. Nearly half of them were Africans, their white teeth contrasting with their dark faces.

The jet taxied down the runway, then came to a stop, and the engine shut off. Dixie undid her seat belt and was one of the first ones at the door. She was so anxious she could hardly wait, but it took a few minutes for the attendant to open it.

The stewardess said, "I hope you had a good flight."

"It was fine!" Dixie flashed her a grin. Then she stepped out of the plane and started down the steps. Her eyes swept the airfield. It looked very small. The buildings here were only one story high, unlike those at the big international airport from which they had taken off.

Almost at once she saw a small group of people waiting behind a fence, and her eyes picked out familiar figures. "Mom— Dad!" she called and waved furiously. They waved back, and she heard their voices calling to her.

Once down the steps, Dixie would have

run to them, but a uniformed attendant said in a strange accent, "Sorry, miss. You must go through Customs."

Dixie had known that but had forgotten.

Clarissa caught up with her, and the two of them went by the Customs desk. But as soon as their bags were checked and she had a nod from the official, Dixie ran through the door. She flew to her mom and dad.

Mr. Morris was not a tall man, but he was well built and sturdy. He picked up Dixie when she flung herself at him, and he hugged her so hard she nearly lost her breath. "Dixie!" he said. "You're here at last!"

"I am, Daddy! I'm here!" When he put her down, her mother embraced her. "Mom, I'm so glad to be here! I've missed you so much!"

"We've missed you, too, sweetheart!" Mrs. Morris was a small woman with light hair and blue eyes, much like Dixie's. She hugged Dixie hard, too.

Dixie saw the tears in her eyes. "Don't cry, Mom," she said. "I'm here now."

"Yes, you are! And I'm never going to let you go again!"

"Where's your companion?" Mr. Morris

15

asked. Then he smiled at Clarissa Harlow. "I'll bet this is Clarissa."

Dixie introduced her parents, and then her dad said, "We know you're both tired after that long flight."

"I am a little bit," Clarissa admitted. "I don't know why, but long flights tire me out worse than work."

"I think it's jet lag," Dixie's mom said. "Well, we're going to take you to the mission station, where you can rest."

Her father said, "I'll take care of the baggage. You three get acquainted."

Twenty minutes later they were driving along the streets in a white Land Rover. Dixie looked around eagerly. She was anxious to learn all she could about her new homeland, Africa. As they pulled up in front of a one-story white stucco building, she said with some disappointment, "But, Dad, where are the lions and all the other animals?"

"There aren't any lions in the big city. But don't worry. You'll see plenty of them."

"When will we be going to our house?"

"Early in the morning. We'll get Miss Clarissa settled here, and then tomorrow first thing, we'll be off."

"Is it far to Tanzania?" Dixie asked.

"It'll take us at least three days," her mother said. "You'll get to see a lot of the country on the way."

The Morrises made sure that Clarissa was settled in her new home. Mr. Morris introduced her to the head of the mission, a tall man with white hair, and then they took Dixie on a tour of the city.

Later that night, they went back to the mission headquarters, where Dixie had her own room. They were served a fine supper —although some of the food was strange— and then she sat with her parents in their bedroom. The three of them talked until Dixie's eyes grew heavy. She had chattered like a magpie, telling all that had happened at the circus and during the time she was with Uncle Roy and Aunt Edith.

At last her mother said, "Dixie, you're falling asleep. Go to bed. We'll have lots of time to hear all of your experiences."

"Time is one thing we do have in Tanzania," Mr. Morris put in. "There's not much to do for entertainment, Dixie. It'll be different for you. Very different from what you've known."

"I don't care!" Dixie said stubbornly.

She smiled. "As long as I'm with you, everything's all right." Then she had a sudden thought. "Oh, I forgot! I brought presents for you!" She ran to her room and was soon back with two small packages. "I couldn't carry much, but I wanted to bring you something from London."

Mr. Morris unwrapped his package. It was a biography of Dwight L. Moody, a man that he had always admired. "This is a book I've always wanted! How'd you know that, Dixie?"

"Well, you didn't tell me more than a hundred times," she said, laughing.

Mrs. Morris unwrapped her package and pulled out a multicolored silk bandanna.

"It was made in India," Dixie said.

"It's beautiful! I wear bandannas a lot out in the sun. Thank you, Dixie."

"Didn't you get yourself anything?" her dad asked.

"Yes, I got this. See." Dixie held out the necklace with the green stone, and her parents admired it.

"That's a very beautiful necklace," her mom said. "I'd like to have one just like it."

"You can have this one, Mom."

"No, you bought us both presents, and

the necklace will be something to remind you of your time in England."

"I'm going to keep it always."

"Well, go to bed now, and early in the morning we'll be on our way."

Over the next two days, they traveled through different kinds of country. Some was mountainous. Some roads ran like a snake through jungle territory. They stopped at night in the homes of villagers that Dixie's parents knew.

On the third night, Dixie was awakened by what sounded like something huge coughing out in the dark. She sat up, remembering. Her father had told her that lions coughed like that. She sat very still and then, suddenly, heard a mighty roaring. Dixie dove down under the covers.

The next morning at breakfast, she said, "Dad, I think I heard a lion last night."

"Probably. There was one prowling around. They're very common in this part of the continent."

"Will there be any where we're going?"

"Oh, yes," he said. "Lots of them. Eat up, now. We ought to be home by late this afternoon."

It was a hard day's journey, but by the time the sun was starting to go down, Mrs. Morris said, "Look, Dixie. There's the village —through those trees—and there's our house!"

Dixie sat up straight and stared at the house where she probably would be spending the next few years. She saw that it was built of timbers, and her father had told her that such houses were rare. Most houses here were made of saplings with mud on top.

Dixie scrambled out of the car, and she and her mother went inside. It was a pleasant house. There was one large room used as a cooking, dining, and living room. There was a small study for her father, a bedroom for her parents, and a bedroom for herself. Almost the first thing Dixie noticed was that there were bars on all the windows.

"What are the bars for? To keep burglars out?"

"No, to keep leopards out," her dad said.

Dixie gave him a startled glance.

"Leopards are worse than lions. They seem to kill for the pure joy of it. One of our best families here lost a child a couple of years ago. A leopard just came in and took the baby off."

Dixie looked at the iron bars and thought soberly, *Wow! This is a different kind of world! We never had to put bars on our windows back home to keep leopards out!*

# 3

# A DIFFERENT KIND OF CHURCH

**S**omething was trying to get in the window!

Dixie usually woke up slowly, but she had slept fitfully her first night in her new home. She had dropped off at last, only to wake up several times. And then a scratching sound caused her eyes to fly open. Now she lay stiffly in the bed, ready to cry out. She just *knew* that something was trying to get into her room.

She remembered the stories about leopards her father had told her. But she said to herself, *There are bars on the windows. Nothing can get in here.*

Nevertheless, the sound continued. It was like fingers scraping against a wall. Finally, she sat bolt upright and stared across the room. Her small single bed was directly across from the window. Slowly Dixie got out of bed. The floorboards were cool under her bare feet.

Taking a deep breath, she whispered, "I've ridden on the back of a tiger. Why should I be afraid of whatever's out there?" Gritting her teeth, she tiptoed toward the window and looked outside. The bright moon painted the whole landscape a ghostly silver. The trees away from the house were moving in the slight breeze as if they were waving. Cautiously Dixie leaned forward until her face was almost even with the bars.

And then she saw it. Down below, a *goat* was grazing. From time to time he would bump against the house with his horns.

Relief ran through her. "I guess that shows how foolish I am," she murmured. She went back to bed.

But for a long time Dixie lay awake, listening to the strange sounds of the African night. Some far-off bird was calling, *"Kula—kula—kula,"* and once she heard a wild laugh. *That must be a hyena. Dad said hyenas sound a lot like somebody laughing.*

Eventually, she dropped off again and knew nothing until a tapping on her door brought her out of sound sleep. When she sat up, rubbing her eyes, she saw her mother, standing fully dressed.

"Get up, sleepyhead!" She came over and kissed Dixie and hugged her. "Your first breakfast in your new home!"

"I want to cook it, Mom! I'm a good cook! Really I am!"

"You can help, but first get dressed."

Dixie leaped out of bed and grabbed her clothes. The bathroom was fitted with an interesting shower. The water had to be pumped into a tank overhead. It was not heated, but it was almost as warm as if it had been. She was to discover that the water here never got cold. This place was near the equator, and temperatures were much higher than she was used to.

She let the tepid water run down over her and quickly completed her shower. Then she put on khaki shorts, a yellow T-shirt, and a pair of sandals. After giving her hair a few strokes, she went into the living area, where she found her dad seated on the couch, reading his new book.

Dixie gave him a kiss. "Good morning, Daddy."

"Good morning, sweetheart." He grinned. "Say, this book is good!"

"Do you really like it?"

"I've always admired D. L. Moody. I think he's one of the greatest men who ever lived. And you know, he was not at all educated. But he said nobody had yet seen what God could do with a man who was totally surrendered to Him. And he wanted to be that man."

"I want to read it when you're through."

"I think you should. It ought to be required reading for every youngster."

When Dixie went over to the kitchen side, her mother said, "I'll let you decide on the first breakfast in your new home."

"Can we have bacon and eggs in Africa?"

"Bacon and eggs coming up! We keep our own little flock of chickens. And that'll be one of your chores—to take care of them."

"Oh, that'll be fun. Do I get to gather the eggs, too?"

"You do. We have to keep the chickens in a cage—or something would run off with them. The villagers have a hard time keeping chickens. We are teaching them how to keep them cooped up. They'd never done that before, but those who try it find that they have a lot better luck keeping them alive."

Her mother set the table, and Dixie threw herself into cooking. She considered herself an expert. She had cooked for Aunt Sarah while she was with the circus, and she had cooked for Uncle Roy and Aunt Edith while she was in the country. Soon the smell of frying bacon was in the air.

When breakfast was ready, her mother said, "You *have* become a good cook!"

"Come on, Dad. It's time to eat," Dixie called.

Mr. Morris asked the blessing. Then, when Dixie filled his plate with three fried eggs and five pieces of bacon, he grinned and said, "You must think I'm starving!"

Dixie enjoyed eating breakfast with her parents. She listened to them talk about the village, about the people there, about the work of the mission. She knew that soon she would know all the African people whose names they mentioned. They sounded so strange to her—not at all like American names.

"Will I learn their language, Dad?" she asked.

"I hope so. It's Swahili. And it's harder than anything *I've* ever tried to learn, but, yes, I think you should learn it."

"Boys and girls always pick up languages quickly. You'll learn a lot from Wamba and Laski."

"Who's that?"

"They are Chief Tombono's children," her father replied. "Wamba's close to your age, and Laski is ten. They're very bright children."

"They've picked up so much *English*," her mother put in. "So quickly it's almost unbelievable. And they love Sunday school."

They sat at the table for a long time, her parents drinking coffee, Dixie sipping hot chocolate, and all talking.

Then Mrs. Morris said, "Let me get the dishes washed, and then we'll go into the village and introduce you to some of the people. You'll have to put on heavier shoes, though. Those sandals won't do."

Dixie put on the pair of Dr. Martens that she treasured, then went back to help her mother finish cleaning up.

The village was not far away, and there was a path to it through the trees. When they arrived, Dixie cried, "What funny-looking houses!" The houses were all low and round and very small. They certainly looked strange. "Does the whole family live inside one of those little things?"

"Yes, they do. They're not like American houses, inside or out," her father answered. "And I'll tell you something else odd about them."

"What's that?"

"The *women* build the houses here."

"The women!" Dixie was astonished. "Don't the men build the houses like they do back home?"

"Not out here. Men do the hunting and take care of the herds. As soon as a girl gets married, she builds her own house."

"That's a funny thing!" Dixie exclaimed. "I wouldn't know how to start."

"Well, a good friend of ours has just gotten married, and she is working on her new home. We'll introduce you to her."

As they walked into the village, Dixie was aware that people were examining her. She whispered, "They're so *tall!*"

"The Masai are a very tall race," her mother said. "And a very proud race, too. They have kept to the old ways more than any other people in Africa."

"I've read a little bit about them." Dixie was looking back at the black faces that stared at her. Both men and women wore sort of robes draped around their shoulders. Some of the women had on ornate jewelry made of beads. "They were very fierce warriors, weren't they?"

"The fiercest in Africa, according to history. Nobody could stand before them. With their broad-headed spears and their courage and strength, they conquered most of this part of the continent."

"Do they still fight?"

"Not anymore. Sometimes they still hunt lions—although it's against regulations."

"Here is the girl I told you about, Dixie," her dad said.

Dixie accompanied her parents up to a framework of sticks half covered with mud. Then they waited until a big woman wearing a red-and-white wrapping turned to them.

She had bracelets on her forearms and wrists and around her neck. Her hair was very short, and her skin was chocolate brown. She had tribal tattoos on her face. She smiled broadly when Mrs. Morris said, "Mana, I want you to meet our daughter, Dixie."

Mana looked down at Dixie from her great height. She was at least six feet tall. She said something in Swahili, and Dixie said, "I'm pleased to meet you, Mana."

Mrs. Morris said something in Swahili to Mana, then turned to Dixie. "I've told her that you are interested in her new home. So she's going to tell you about it, and I'll interpret."

Mana seemed very proud of her house. She talked, and Dixie's mom told Dixie what she said. "This is my house. I will build it myself. First, I gather long tree branches and stick them in the earth. Then I tie them together with vines and fill in the open spaces with leaves and grass." She showed Dixie the outside of the house.

Dixie asked, "Is that mud that you're covering it with?"

"No. That is cow dung."

Dixie glanced at her parents, who were grinning.

"That's right. They use cow dung to plaster the outside of their houses."

"But won't so much cow dung smell bad?"

"It may to you or me," her dad said, "but they don't seem to mind it."

"I guess it's whatever a person gets used to," Dixie said with a gulp.

There was a strong smell about the whole village, anyway, for there were no sewers. She guessed she would get used to this, but right now it was a bit sickening. She watched Mana spread more cow dung.

Mana said, "My house will be better than most houses. I have thought about it for a long time. It must be weatherproof. Before the rainy season, I must patch it again so that there are no cracks. I will show you the inside."

Dixie stepped inside and saw that the house would be mostly one large room.

"This is the guest bed," Mana said. It consisted of a platform of sticks with a grass mattress. "This is the mother's bed. My bed when I have little ones," she said. "Here is firewood. And this is where I will cook."

The hearth was in the middle of the room. Dixie asked, "Doesn't it get smoky?"

The question seemed to puzzle Mana. "Fire makes smoke," she said.

Mrs. Morris interpreted that. "It doesn't seem to bother them. The smoke winds its way out."

"What is this little room here for?"

"Ah!" Mana smiled. "This is where we keep the newborn calves so they will be safe. And this is for baby goats and sheep." That was another little compartment. Mana was obviously very proud of her house. "Soon," she said, "I will be in. Then you will come and visit me."

"I will, Mana." Dixie asked her mother how to say, "I'm pleased to meet you," in Swahili. She listened carefully, then repeated the phrase to Mana, who happily assured Dixie again that she would be glad to have her visit her new home when it was finished.

After they left Mana's house-building, Mrs. Morris said, "Now we want you to meet the chief."

They walked then to a house in the center of the village. She saw, standing in front of it, a tall, strongly built man who had an ornate tattoo on his face. He wore on his head the mane of a black lion.

"Chief Tombono, this is my daughter, Dixie," Mr. Morris said.

"A girl child," Tombono said in English. "You come from across the water."

"Yes, Chief Tombono," Dixie said. She

thought she should bow. He was an impressive looking man. "I am glad to be here with my father and mother."

Tombono considered her, then said, "It is good for a girl to be with her parents."

"You speak English very well."

Just then a woman, a boy, and a girl came out. The woman too was tall. She had warm eyes, and her hair was fixed in rolls held in place by clay and cow dung. She had scars in fancy patterns all over her body. She spoke less English than the chief, but she had a warm smile for Dixie.

"This is Chief Tombono's wife, Minna, and this is Wamba," Mrs. Morris said. "He is the son of the chief."

"One day he will be chief," Tombono said proudly.

Wamba was lean but tall. He had only one tribal marking on his face. He said, "Hello," just as an American boy would.

"I'm glad to meet you, Wamba," Dixie said.

"This is my sister, Laski."

Laski was small and quick.

"I hope we'll be good friends," Dixie said to them.

"We come to Sunday school and hear about Jesus God," Wamba said.

But when he said this, Dixie saw a frown form on the chief's face. She glanced at her father, but he closed his lips and gave her a shake of his head. *I'll have to ask him about that later,* she thought.

"Why don't you two show Dixie around the village and introduce her? Will that be all right, Chief?"

Tombono gave Dixie a close look. "Yes." Then he turned and walked away.

As Dixie, Wamba, and Laski began their tour of the village, Dixie said with some hesitation, "I'm . . . I'm not sure your father likes me."

Wamba and Laski exchanged glances.

"Our father, he does not like Jesus God," Wamba said.

"Oh!" Dixie said faintly. "I'm sorry to hear that!"

"But *we* do," Laski said. "Your mother teaches us many things in Sunday school."

Wamba nodded shortly but did not say anything more.

The tour of the village was interesting. Dixie met many of the villagers. Some boys and girls joined them. By the time they started back to Wamba and Laski's home, there was quite a parade.

Suddenly Laski whispered something in Swahili to Wamba.

The boy turned to Dixie. His brown eyes were hooded. "Maugombo over there," he said.

"Who's he?"

"Witch doctor."

Dixie had heard of scary stories of witch doctors. But when they neared the man, she was startled to see that Maugombo was old, small, and scrawny. He wore oversized frames of glasses with no glass in them. He had on a bushy headdress, a necklace of lions' teeth, and a lion skin around his waist. His eyes were cold and penetrating as he looked at Dixie. He did not speak to her, and she did not speak to him.

After they had passed by, Dixie said, "Wamba, that man—Maugombo—he scares me a little bit."

"Very powerful man," Wamba said quietly.

One other disturbing thing happened on the tour. An elderly Masai woman offered Dixie a gift. She saw how poor the woman was, and she refused it.

At once Wamba said in English, "Take it! You have insulted her!"

"Oh, I'm sorry!"

Laski said, "When someone offers you a gift, always take it. To say no is to insult them."

Dixie at once reached out and took the woman's present—it was a small carved stone—and she said quickly, "Tell her how much I appreciate it. Shall I give her something?"

"That would be good," Wamba said.

Dixie reached into her pocket and took out a small mirror. She gave it to the old woman, who looked in it with great delight. She had lost most of her teeth, but she seemed to find herself very attractive.

They walked on. Soon they came to an open place, and Laski said, "See. We have church now."

It was a weekday, not a Sunday, and the "church" was very different from any that Dixie had ever attended. In the first place, it was outdoors, which was strange. And no one sat down. They all stood as they listened to the preacher—who was her father.

The women stood on one side, the very

young people stood in the back, and there were two groups of men.

"Why are the men separated from each other?" she whispered to Laski.

"The young ones are the warriors," Laski whispered back. "The older ones are the elders."

"One day I will be an elder," Wamba said proudly, "but I will be a warrior first."

The sermon was in Swahili, so Dixie could not understand it. Wamba interpreted some of it for her, however. "He is telling about Jesus. How He went about doing good. Now he is telling how Jesus healed a blind man—gave him sight."

The sermon went on awhile. Since Dixie could not understand the words, she watched the faces around her. Chief Tombono had not come to the service, at least not formally. She saw, however, that he was at the edge of the crowd, standing in a strange fashion on one leg. His other foot was braced against his knee, and he balanced himself with a large staff. He did not appear to be listening. But once he turned his head, and Dixie met his eyes, and she knew that he was.

Her father didn't preach long. After the

preaching, he talked to different people, and Wamba told Dixie what was being said.

Then the chief came up to him. "Jesus God you preach. Was He a warrior?"

Her father seemed to know exactly what was in the man's mind. The Masai respected strength and physical courage. The chief would have no respect for even Jesus if He were not strong.

"Yes," Mr. Morris said. "He was God's warrior. He gave His life for His people."

Chief Tombono's dark face did not change. He stared at the missionary, then turned and walked away without another word.

"He's a hard case," Dixie's dad said quietly. "He's been told about the spirits— the gods of his people—all his life. He can't understand a God of love."

Dixie looked after the tall form of the chief, and she whispered, "I think his children understand some."

"Yes," her father said. "They do. And someday Chief Tombono will know the God of love as well."

# 4

# DIXIE MAKES A TRADE

Almost a week went by. Dixie quickly settled into life at the mission. It was indeed different. One thing she noticed was that none of the Masai had a watch.

"These people have no sense of time—not like we do," her mother told her. "Their clock is the sky. When the sun comes up, it's time to get up. When it goes down, it's time to go to bed. They don't have any meetings to go to. Except for the elders, perhaps. Life just goes on. There's no sense trying to hurry them. We found that out."

"It's so different here!" Dixie exclaimed.

"It certainly is. At home, when church starts at ten o'clock, we expect people to be there. But here, when we go out to a village and announce a meeting, we get to the place and nobody's there. At first that bothered us. But we learned to sit around and wait, and then maybe an hour later one person would come, or two. Then half an hour later, more would come. Finally, after a long time, a crowd would gather."

"They don't care how long the sermons are, either."

"No, it's a nice break in their lives. Are you very bored here, Dixie?"

"No, Mom. I'm learning so much."

"You're certainly picking up Swahili quickly."

"It's so hard. It's not at all like English."

"I know. But keep listening to it all you can. You'll find out you will pick up some of it without even trying."

"You know what I miss most out here, Mom?"

"What?"

"Diet Cokes!"

Mrs. Morris broke out in a laugh. "I know what you mean. When I first got here, I found I could put up with any of the inconveniences, but I missed Snickers candy bars. Oh, how I longed for Snickers, just the way you do for Diet Cokes!"

"Maybe after a while you just forget about them."

"I'd still like to have a Snickers."

Dixie grinned at her mother. "And I'd still like to have a Diet Coke. But I can get along without it. I think I'll go for a walk."

"All right, but don't go wandering too far away."

"Oh, I won't!"

Dixie enjoyed walking around the village. She could see the mountains rising far over to the east. She had learned that the Swahili called them the Mountains of God.

She had not gone far before Wamba joined her. He wore a simple piece of cloth draped over his shoulder and knotted around his waist. She greeted him warmly. "Hello, Wamba."

"Hello, Dixie. Going for a walk?"

"Yes."

"I will go with you. I will show you the ants."

"The ants?"

"Yes. You must see where the ants live."

Dixie could not understand what would be so fascinating about ants. But she went along with him.

They walked until they came to some small hills. But when Dixie looked closer, she saw that these were, indeed, *ant*hills. "I never saw anything like that!"

"The ants fly once a year. The air is thick with them. They leave in the morning and fly as far as they can. Then their wings drop off. You have to keep your mouth shut, or they'll fly right in." Wamba grinned at her expression. "They don't taste as good as zebra."

"Well, I've never eaten zebra, but I don't want to eat any ants!"

He laughed at her. "You are funny about what you eat. The Masai are much simpler."

"What's your favorite kind of food?"

"Milk," Wamba said. "We like milk best of all."

"I like milk, too."

"It's best with a little cow blood in it."

Dixie looked at him with amazement. *"Blood?"*

"Did you not know that? You open the vein of the cow and let it bleed a little into the milk." He rubbed his stomach and smacked his lips. "Very good!"

"I'm sure it is," Dixie said weakly. But she made up her mind that was one delicacy of Africa that she would definitely *not* try.

As they went along, Wamba pointed out different kinds of birds. She knew the kingfishers. Then he pointed out a huge eagle. "That one is almost big enough to carry off a lamb," he said.

They saw doves and then a bird with a huge bill. "That looks like a hornbill," she said. "I've seen their picture."

"In Swahili his name means big nose."

They were now in a more heavily vegetated area. Dixie had just started to comment, "It's so hot here—" when she screamed and leaped wildly backward, falling against Wamba. "A snake!" she shrieked.

Wamba held Dixie to keep her from falling. Then he looked down and laughed again. "That's only a pig snake," he said. "He's a good fellow."

Dixie looked at the thick-bodied snake. She looked at its large head. It looked fierce indeed.

"He hisses and puffs and blows, but he won't hurt you."

"He looks like he would."

"I will teach you which snakes are good and which are bad."

As they walked on, he described some of the bad snakes.

Dixie became quite jumpy. "Let's not talk about snakes anymore." She shivered. "I can't stand them."

Wamba looked at her with surprise. "But your father says that God made all things. He made snakes—even those you call bad ones."

"I know," Dixie said. "Never could understand why He made things like mosquitoes and poisonous snakes. But I know He did."

Dixie found herself liking Wamba very much. Today he told her about many things. After a while, however, he grew quiet. Together they sat beside a small stream. He picked up a stick, began to dabble it in the water, and fell utterly silent.

Dixie knew something was troubling him. "What's the matter, Wamba?"

The boy did not answer for a while, then he looked up at her. "It is my father."

"What's wrong with him? Isn't he good to you?"

"He loves me very much. I am his only son. One day I will be the chief, and he puts all his hopes and his dreams in me."

"Then what's the matter?"

Wamba looked away and seemed embarrassed. He broke the stick in two and threw it out into the water. He watched it pulled downstream. He muttered, "He no like Jesus God."

"I know that. It's too bad. But he can change, Wamba."

Then Wamba turned back to her, and she saw a strange light in his eyes. "I like Jesus God. I love Him. Your father tells me all about how He died for me. How could I not love one who would die for me? But my father thinks the spirits of Maugombo—the old gods—are stronger."

"I'm glad you're a Christian, Wamba," Dixie said. "That means we're brother and sister—that's what the Bible says."

Wamba's white teeth flashed. "You are my sister?"

"Not like Laski is your sister. But all Christians—no matter what color they are or where they are from—are really brothers and sisters in the Lord."

"That is good. I like you for a sister."

"Don't worry about your father. We'll pray for him, and one day he'll become a believer, too. What about your mother?"

"She must do what my father says. It is the way of our people."

Dixie was not sure this was a good way, but she determined to say nothing. Her parents had cautioned her again and again not to try to force her beliefs on the Masai.

Dixie and Wamba played in the water for a long time. She thought, *I'm having fun with Wamba just as I did with my friends back in America. His color doesn't make any difference at all.*

They took a different route going home. By and by they came to an old hut that was almost falling in, and Dixie asked who lived there.

"Old man. He is very . . ." Wamba paused, then shrugged. "He is old and not happy."

Dixie wanted to know more about the old man. But once again, she did not ask questions. As they were passing the house, she heard a sound. She turned and saw something that made her eyes fly open. "It's a cheetah!"

"Yes, a cub. Lots of them around here."

"But look at him!" Dixie said. "He's being choked by that chain. And he's so skinny!"

Wamba said, "He will maybe not live. The old man—Tombu—he is not kind."

"What's he going to do with a cheetah?"

"Maybe try to sell him to traders. Sometimes they buy animals when they come through."

"I want to look at him. Would it be all right?"

Wamba was a little cautious. "He is a mean man, Tombu, but we will see."

They approached the hut.

The man came out. He was thin and unhealthy looking, unlike most of the Masai. He also looked very old. He spoke sharply to them.

Dixie didn't understand a word, but she knew he meant for them to be off.

Wamba explained that Dixie wanted to look at the cub. The old man glared at her and said something more.

"It's all right to look," Wamba said, "but not to stay long."

The cub was tied to a tree. The rusty chain around his neck was fastened much too tightly. The cheetah was about half-grown.

Wamba said, "He may bite!"

Dixie knelt down and waited. She had learned from her experience with the circus never to rush an animal.

The cheetah's head, as with all cheetahs, seemed oversized. He stood cautiously watching her with his enormous eyes.

Slowly Dixie extended her hand. She was ready to jerk it back, although she knew he would be too fast for her.

The cheetah did not move, and Dixie did not attempt to touch him. But finally he thrust his head forward a fraction and smelled her fingers. Dixie talked to him quietly.

"He's so thin. I bet he hasn't had enough to eat in a long time. And see—he's out of water."

"The old man doesn't care much about animals. He's had several, and most of them have died from lack of care."

Dixie suddenly knew that she could not let that happen! *I've got to do something!* she thought. She said, "Ask him if he will sell the cheetah."

Wamba put the question to Tombu, and the old man shook his head. "He doesn't want to sell him."

"But he's poor, isn't he?"

"Yes, he is."

"I'll bet he would sell if I could find something he wanted. Ask him if there's anything that he wants that I could get him."

Wamba spoke in Swahili for some time. He talked for so long that Dixie knew that he was trying to persuade the old man and was not being successful.

Suddenly Dixie stepped up directly in front of the man. "Please," she said. "I'll give you anything I can."

Wamba translated this.

Without warning, Tombu reached out and touched the green stone of her necklace. He spoke, and Wamba interpreted. "He will take the necklace for the cub."

"Oh!" Dixie had wanted to keep the necklace forever. But she could not let the cub suffer. "All right," she said. She slipped off the necklace and handed it to the old Masai.

He took it, sniffed, and then went back into the hut, fastening the necklace around his neck.

"Well, I've got a cheetah," Dixie said.

"You think your parents will let you keep him?"

"I don't know. I hope they will. Do you think we can get him home?"

That did not prove to be difficult. The

young cheetah sat patiently while Dixie carefully undid the short chain from about the tree. She would use it as a lead.

"You'll have to bring the chain back after you get him home," Wamba advised.

Dixie soon found that the cheetah would follow her if she gently tugged on the chain. Walking close to her, he seemed very tall. But he was nothing but skin and bones.

"Cheetahs are very fast," Wamba said at one point. "Nothing can catch them."

The two made their way back to Dixie's house. When her parents came outside, Mr. Morris took one look at the cheetah and said, "Oh no! Where'd you get *that*?"

"I traded my necklace for him. Look, he's starving. He was going to die."

"I don't think keeping a cheetah is a good idea, Dixie," her mother said. "You don't know anything about them. They get quite big. And they're a wild animal."

"But I was with wild animals in the circus. And I'll take care of him. I promise. You won't ever have to worry about him."

A family conference took place with Wamba standing to one side. Dixie begged and pleaded. And when her parents finally gave in, she gave a sigh of relief.

She knelt and put her arm around the cheetah. "I'm going to call you Flash," she whispered. "And we're going to be great friends!"

## 5
# STRONG MEDICINE

**D**ixie gasped, then stumbled, then cried, *"Ngoja kidogo!"* It was one of the Swahili phrases she had memorized. It meant "Wait a little!"

Wamba, who had been running ahead of her, stopped and turned around. He grinned while she stood gasping for breath. *"L'ojuju mali,"* he said.

Dixie knew that *L'ojuju* was the Swahili word for "white person." It literally meant "the hairy one." But she did not know the meaning of the other word.

He added, "That means white skins are weaker than black skins."

"You just wait," Dixie said, glaring at him. "Give me a little time, and I'll keep up with you."

Wamba slowed his pace as they walked

across the plain. The level land was covered with grass that came up almost to Dixie's waist at times. Dotted here and there were the umbrella trees, odd-shaped trees that seemed to be pressed down on the top by a giant hand.

Far off to her right, she could see dust, and she asked, "What's that, Wamba?"

"*Dong-go-ko*. Zebra running fast."

"Oh, I want to see them!"

Wamba had quickly become Dixie's guide for the territory that surrounded the village. Both he and Laski had spent innumerable hours wandering the countryside with her. He always seemed amused that she wanted to see every kind of animal.

As they tramped toward the zebra herd, now standing still on the plain, she asked him the Swahili words for different things. Dixie had a good memory and was good at learning languages, so she was already making progress. But she just could not make some of the sounds that the Masai made very easily. One in particular called for a clicking sort of sound way back in the throat. So far, she had not mastered that.

Once she pointed at a delicate blue flower and asked, "How do you say that?"

"It is called *waguna*." He listened as Dixie said the word, and then he howled. "What you just said was, 'The monkey died.'"

"Oh, fudge!" Dixie exclaimed. "I'll never learn this language."

"You will. You do very well for a *L'ojuju*."

Dixie had learned that the Masai called themselves simply "the people," as if there were no other people in the whole world— or as if all other human beings were something other than *people*. But her father told her that most people think their own race is better than anybody else's.

They came closer to the zebras, and Wamba said, "Maybe we see one of them taken."

"By a cheetah?"

"No. Cheetahs usually eat only smaller animals—antelope maybe. No. Lions or hyenas, they eat zebras."

Dixie had seen a cheetah run down an antelope in a nature movie back in the States. She had little desire to see that side of life. But she had already learned that in Africa people looked at life differently. Every day there was death before their eyes, either of animals or of humans.

Wamba suddenly swerved aside and

pulled up a small plant. He was carefully putting it into the leather bag at his side when Dixie asked, "What's that, Wamba?"

"*Ol-umigumi.*"

"Is it good to eat?"

"No. Eat with meat before lion hunt. It gives a warrior courage."

"Have you ever seen a lion killed with a spear?"

"Four times. Once my father killed one."

"I don't see how anyone can stand up to a wild lion with only a spear."

"All Masai warriors must hunt lions."

"Do many of them get killed?"

"Some. Others get badly hurt. Only those who kill the lion can wear the lion-mane headdress such as my father wears."

Suddenly the zebra herd seemed to explode. There was a low thundering sound, and the mass of black-and-white stripes blurred before Dixie's eyes.

"There! See?"

Dixie squinted. She saw some sort of commotion at the rear of the herd. "What is it?"

"Lion takes a zebra. Other lions come now. See?"

But Dixie had little desire to see the lions at their bloody feast, so she turned away and said, "Let's go home."

As they walked back, she listened to Wamba tell more about his people. He knew much of their history through their songs and through the stories that the elders told.

They were almost home again when suddenly a strange looking animal emerged from a burrow and scurried in front of them.

"What's that? It looks like an armadillo." Actually Dixie was to find out that it was a pangolin, a cousin of the armadillo often found in southwestern United States. The two youngsters ran after it, and Dixie noticed that it had overlapping armor on its back and legs and tail.

"If I were a warrior, I would kill it," Wamba said.

"Are they good to eat?"

"Not really good. But warriors know that its plates will bring good luck in love to the one who wears them."

When Dixie laughed aloud, he stared at her suspiciously. "What is funny?"

"Oh, it's nothing! Back home, though,

a boy takes a girl some flowers or something sweet to eat. He wouldn't think of wearing part of a dead animal."

"Your people do not know much, do they?"

Then they came to the river that circled the village, and Dixie said, "Let's sit down and rest awhile. I want to dabble my feet in the water."

She sat on the bank, took off her shoes, and put her feet in the stream. The water was warm, and the brown mud oozed up between her toes. It felt good. She sat there dreamily while Wamba wandered off down the river, looking for signs of river birds. He'd said he was learning to shoot them with his arrows for their plumage.

Dixie sat thinking over her time in Africa. She had learned so much! It would be a long time before she could speak the Masai language, but she certainly was learning how different the people were.

She remembered old Tombu, from whom she had bought Flash. She'd taken him a cake she had baked, and he'd begun eating without a word of thanks. But she went back twice—and the last time, he invited her to sit down! Using Laski as an interpreter, she talked with him for a long time. When they left, she said, "I thought he was just mean, Laski. But he's sad, isn't he? All of his family are dead, and he's all alone."

"He *is* lonely. It is good that you come and visit him."

She had become good friends with most of the youngsters in the village and could call all of their names now. She was teaching them games such as Red Rover and Hide and Seek, which they delighted in playing.

The day was hot. Flies buzzed around as usual, and she brushed them aside. There was no avoiding flies in Africa. Seeing a baby with its eyes ringed with flies always gave Dixie a bad feeling. She knew the child's eyes would become infected. Her parents were trying to introduce the use of medicine to help, but many people preferred the charms from Maugombo to the white man's medicine.

Suddenly a strong hand jerked Dixie to her feet and dragged her backward. At the same time she heard Wamba shouting her name. Then she found herself thrown over a wide black shoulder. She thought she was being kidnapped.

With a splash, a huge crocodile surfaced! She saw Wamba running beside her now, and she caught one more glimpse of the crocodile. It was covering the ground toward them much faster than she would have thought possible.

But the strong arm around her tightened, and her rescuer quickly carried her away from the scaly monster.

Then the man put her down, and with a gasp she looked up to see Chief Tombono. He was looking at her with a strange expression. "You make a good meal for crocodile," he said.

A shiver ran over Dixie as she thought how close she had come to death. "Oh, Chief," she said, "you saved my life!"

"White girl is foolish to dangle her feet in the river. Foolish!" He turned and stiffly walked away.

"I thought it was just a *log!*" Dixie said.

"A log with big teeth. You wouldn't be the first to be snapped up by *dalenu*. He's the boss of the river. Like the elephant's boss of the land. Let's go home."

The day after Dixie's narrow escape from the crocodile, she and Laski stopped off to see Mana, whose house was progressing. They even helped her for a while by gathering grass to put between the upright sticks.

"It's almost finished," Mana said. "You are good to help me." This, of course, was interpreted by Laski. But Dixie was able to say a phrase that Laski had taught her. "Much happiness to you, and may you have many children."

Mana grinned and nodded vigorously.

Then the girls left. They had gone only a short way when they found Wamba taking his cows out to pasture. It was the job of the boys to care for the cattle.

The life of a Masai boy, Dixie had discovered, was well ordered. Every male Masai passed through three main stages in life—first, boyhood; then, warriorhood; then, elderhood. She also found out that in some complicated way the warriors were subdivided into junior and senior warriors.

Dixie was walking and listening to Wamba talk about this. As always, she was fascinated to hear anything concerning the Masai. She stopped short, however, when she saw a little boy lying on the ground outside a hut.

"What's wrong with him?"

"Sick. Very sick."

Dixie hesitated.

A woman was crouched beside the boy. She was watching Dixie.

Dixie edged forward, nodding and giving the Masai greeting. *"Ibubu."*

The woman nodded back.

With the help of Wamba, Dixie started a conversation. "I'm sorry your child is sick."

"Very sick. Very sick. Will die."

The calmness with which the woman spoke shook Dixie. Back in the States, such a sick child would have been rushed to a hospital. There would have been doctors and medicines and all sorts of care. But here the mother simply sat doing nothing, for there was nothing to do.

Dixie gently put her hand on the boy's forehead. "He has fever."

"Very sick," the mother repeated.

A thought came to Dixie. "Come on, Wamba," she said. "I'm going to get some aspirin."

As they went to her house, she explained what aspirin was and what it did. They soon came back with some. Through

Wamba, she explained to the mother that the medicine would help make the boy's fever go away.

At that moment, Maugombo, the witch doctor, appeared from between two of the huts. He glared at Dixie as he came toward them. Then he spoke swiftly in Swahili.

The woman replied, keeping her eyes down.

Wamba said nothing.

When Dixie looked at him, she saw that he too had his eyes turned away.

"Maugombo," she said, holding up the bottle, "this medicine is good. It will help the child."

But when Wamba translated for her, the witch doctor struck her hand and sent the bottle rolling. He spoke in fierce, fast phrases and almost seemed to be having a fit.

"Come away!" Wamba said quickly. He scooped up the bottle of aspirin and tugged at Dixie's arm, practically dragging her off.

When they were out of hearing, Dixie said angrily, "All the boy has to do is take the aspirin, and at least the fever will go down!"

Wamba did not answer for a long time.

Then he said, "She is afraid of Maugombo. Everybody is."

"Afraid of him! What would he do?"

"He will put a spell on her. A leopard will come and take her—or something else bad will happen."

"But that's foolish, Wamba! You don't believe that, do you?"

When she turned to look at the boy, she realized that he did. And then she remembered the warnings of her parents. *You can't force your Christian beliefs on others.* After all, Wamba had grown up seeing Maugombo and the fear that people had of him and what happened as a result of his "spells."

Wamba at last looked at her. He said, "He has strong medicine."

Dixie knew he did not mean medicine such as the missionary doctors used. They walked for a few steps more, and then she knew she had to say something. "Maybe so, Wamba. Satan has power. But whatever 'medicine' Maugombo has, it's not as strong as Jesus."

Wamba took this in. After a few moments he broke the silence. "Everybody is afraid of Maugombo. He is an evil man. We have seen people die when he puts spells on them. It is not foolishness." He hesitated, then asked, "You think Jesus God is truly stronger?"

"Yes, I do. Jesus is the One who made the world. Everything you see was made by Him. He is almighty God."

Wamba chewed on his lip but did not answer.

And Dixie thought as they moved on, *It's going to take a long time. That Mau-gombo has got everybody under his thumb.*

# 6

# THE FASTEST THING ON FOUR FEET

**E**very day on the mission station seemed the same as every other day. Dixie got up, made breakfast, spent some time with her parents, and then the work began. Her dad and mom were very busy missionaries. They traveled to other villages almost every day. Sometimes she went with them. But if it was a very short trip, she would remain at home.

For entertainment she had a shortwave radio. It could pick up both American and British stations. It was also fascinating to hear stations in Germany and other countries where she did not understand the language. Some programs were in Swahili, and this helped her language study. She spent some time each day studying. Often, Wamba and Laski were her teachers.

She had more time for Bible reading and for thinking about the Lord than she had ever had before. Back in America, so much had been going on that she'd had to squeeze in time to read and think. Here in Africa, she found herself with so much time that some days she could spend as much as two hours simply reading the Bible.

It had become the most wonderful book in the world to her—and this, of course, delighted her parents. She found herself being considered an authority in the village. All her young friends loved to hear her read from the Bible. None of them could read. They were fascinated that those little black marks on the white book paper said something.

Several times a week, Dixie sat under one of the baobab trees while the young boys watched over the cows. She would read stories to them from the Old Testament. Most could understand almost no English, so she would read a sentence and then Wamba or Laski would translate for her. She found that they loved stories of adventure such as Elijah's calling down fire.

When she read the story of the Flood, though, she was met with blank looks.

Wamba said finally, "I cannot explain that to them. Water is in the river. It is not over your head."

Dixie had a difficult time explaining what a flood was. The children all thought it was very funny that water would come up out of the river and flow over one's head.

When she read how Samson, with his bare hands, had killed a lion, Wamba said instantly, "He was a Masai!"

"I guess he was, kind of. He was the strongest man who ever lived."

"And he really had no spear?" he asked suspiciously.

"No spear. The Bible says he just killed it as easily as if it were a small animal."

"I would like to have seen that," Wamba said. "Sometimes it takes five or six strong Masai warriors to overcome a lion. And they all get bitten or clawed. Some badly. I would like to be like this Samson."

Dixie found that they were interested in the miracles too—especially of Jesus walking on the water. When she read that, the children all asked her to read it again.

Laski said, "I would like to have seen *that!* He must have been a God to walk on the water."

"He could outrun a crocodile if He could walk on water," Wamba said. He thought for a moment. "Did *you* ever see anybody walk on water, Dixie?"

"No, I never did. I think that only happened one time and probably will never happen again. After all, this was *Jesus*—not just a man."

And so the days passed for Dixie—learning the language, learning what the people were like, trying to fit herself into their strange customs. Sure enough, she had been offered milk with the blood drawn from a cow and had forced herself to take a small swallow. It would have been ill-mannered to refuse.

When Wamba asked, "How did you like it?" she said, "Very nice," in a rather weak voice. "After all," she told her parents later, "he might not like it if I offered him chicken livers or something else that he's not used to. But I'd want him to be polite."

One Thursday morning, Dixie did the thing that was taking a large part of her time. She went out to where Flash was kept in the large pen that her father had hired two men to build. It was made of strong wire that he had hauled in from the city.

Dixie opened the gate and went inside. Flash nuzzled her as she put down his food. Then she sat beside him and watched him eat daintily. He was bigger and stronger now, no longer the skinny cub that she had rescued.

She stroked his rough fur and talked to him as she often did. "You're getting to be a big boy, Flash. Almost grown. I bet if you were out in the wild, you would have already brought down an antelope all by yourself."

Flash lifted his head. He had been drinking the goat's milk that she had poured for him. He licked his chops and made a purring sound. He was always very friendly and affectionate, and Dixie loved spending hours with him—which she did whenever she didn't have anything else to do. She used to keep him on a leash when he was outside the pen, but he was well trained now and never tried to break away. The villagers had gotten accustomed to him, too. Even some of the dogs, who had barked viciously at the big cat at first, now paid him no attention whatsoever.

For a long time Dixie sat with him. Then she looked up to see Laski turn the corner. "Laski!" she said. "Let's go train Flash."

"All right," Laski said. She was wearing very little in the heat. Her dress was just a twist of cloth that went over one shoulder and came halfway to her knees. She wore two bracelets, one on each forearm, and she looked very pretty. Her hair was done up with mud and cow dung, but Dixie was used to that. She had refused, however, when Laski offered to help her fix her own hair that way.

The two girls left the village with Flash. He sniffed around eagerly. He enjoyed his walks. If he ran off, he would always come back.

Dixie had taught him to come back to her by a very simple process. She carried a leather bag full of bits of the pork that he dearly loved. Laski would hold the cheetah while Dixie went some distance away, holding onto the rope that was around Flash's neck. Dixie then would say, "Come," and pull him toward her. When the cheetah came, she would give him a bit of pork.

Now he always came when called, even without the rope, and she always rewarded him with a piece of pork. "That way," she had told Laski and Wamba, "he'll always come and won't run away."

"I don't think he'd run away, anyhow," Wamba had said. "He's like a big pet. Never saw anything like it—a cheetah that's almost like a house cat."

When they were away from the village, the girls began to do something that Dixie had practiced for some weeks now with Laski's and Wamba's help. She gave the leash to Laski and then trotted until she was about the length of a football field away. "Are you ready?" she called.

"Yes!" Laski yelled back. Then she slipped the leash off Flash's neck.

"Flash! Come *quick!*" Dixie called.

At once the cheetah exploded into a burst of speed. One moment he was standing still, and the next he was covering the ground at a frightening rate. He was nearly a blur as his claws dug into the turf, his long legs stretching out. And almost before Dixie could blink, he stood in front of her.

"Good boy, Flash!" She fed him a piece of pork, and he nudged her, asking for more. But she said, "You've got to work for it. Now, *stay!*"

It had been harder to teach him that

command, but he had finally learned to stay until she called him.

Dixie trotted back to where Laski was standing and then took out a piece of the pork. "Flash! Come!" she yelled.

The cheetah broke into a dead run and was in front of Dixie very quickly.

"He is so fast," Laski said.

"The fastest thing on four legs," Dixie agreed. "I knew that even before I came here. Nothing on four legs can move as fast over a short distance as a cheetah can. Not a horse or anything. Only a bird can fly faster than a cheetah can move."

The two girls had great fun playing with the cheetah, who enjoyed the game, too. Then Dixie said, "Now I'm going to try something new."

"What's that?"

"I'm going to teach him to go home."

"How will you teach him that?"

"Well, we've taught him what 'home' means. Every day when we start back, we say, 'Home.' And yesterday I took him out a ways, and I said, 'Home, Flash!' and he ran right back to his cage!"

"Ooh, he is smart!" Laski said. "But will he wait there for you?"

"He did yesterday. He ran right to the pen and stayed in front of his cage until I got there. Then I fed him. I did that five times, and he always ran right back to his cage and waited there."

"But we're nearly a mile from your house today. Will he do it when he can't see us?"

"I guess we'll see," Dixie said. She had been petting Flash, and now she stood up. She said, "Home, Flash!"

As soon as she spoke, the cheetah was off once again in a blinding flash of speed.

"Let's be sure he goes there," Dixie said. "Come on!"

The two girls ran after Flash as hard as they could, but the cheetah was out of sight before they had gone a hundred yards.

"I sure hope he stays at his cage," Dixie said. "I'd hate for him to go back to the wild."

However, when they got to the house, Flash was sitting calmly in front of his pen. She ran to him and knelt and pulled out all the remaining bits of pork. "Here, you can have it all! You're a good boy, Flash! A good boy!"

Flash daintily ate the meat and then

whined for more. But Dixie said, "No, you're getting to be a pig, but I will get you some goat's milk."

The two girls sat watching the cheetah lap it up. Then he plopped down on the ground and gazed at them sleepily. He always went to sleep after he ate. He looked just like a big cat as he lay there nodding.

Dixie thought back to the time when she had ridden Stripes, the huge Siberian tiger, in the circus. She had loved Stripes with all her heart and thought she would never find another big cat that she would love as well. But as she stroked Flash's head, she said, "I love you as much as I did Stripes."

Flash purred deep in his throat. He was content. He was filled with pork and goat's milk, and Dixie's hand was pleasant on his head.

## 7

# THE TRADER

I t doesn't seem possible I've been here so long."

Dixie was talking to herself as she walked with Flash down along the river. Overhead a few vultures were high specks in the sky. Vultures were always a part of the African landscape.

Dixie, as usual, delighted in watching the cheetah. He would obediently wait until she got almost out of sight, then at her call he would burst into speed, covering the ground like a flying arrow. She carried a pouchful of pork pieces for him.

They had just rounded a bend in the river when suddenly the water churned. Dixie stopped as a herd of hippos whipped the water to a milky froth. She did not know what they were doing, but Wamba had warned her that hippos were very dangerous. "They're faster than you think," he'd said. "And they can bite a crocodile in two with one bite. Stay away from them!"

She watched, fascinated. There were three baby hippos. They looked just like their parents except that they were smaller. They played in the water like seals.

Finally Dixie backed away, so that she avoided being seen by them, and she moved on. During her months in Africa, she had learned much about safety first. She'd been surprised when her father told her that the most dangerous animals for someone caught out after dark were not the lions or the leopards but the hyenas.

"They hunt in packs. And they actually have the strongest jaws of any animal. They look ridiculous, but they're really *very* dangerous."

Dixie had no intention of being caught out after dark. She was always at home when the sun went down.

She arrived at the village at the time Wamba with the other boys was bringing the cows back from grazing. They were huge animals. Some of them had sweeping horns. The owner of each cow had branded her with a particular sign so that, no matter how far they went, ownership was certain.

"Hello, Dixie," Wamba greeted her.

"I've been out by the river. I saw some baby hippos," she said. "They're so cute."

"You think everything's cute. Even wart-hogs."

"Well, they are!" she argued. "They're so ugly they're cute!"

Wamba laughed at her as he often did. "I found something I want to show you," he said.

"Don't you have to watch the cows?"

"No." He turned and said something to his friends. They laughed at him and said something in Swahili that Dixie did not catch.

"What did they say?" she asked.

Wamba grinned. "They said I spend so much time with you that I'm going to turn into a white girl."

"That's silly!"

"I know. They're a silly bunch, those boys. They don't have near the wisdom that I have."

"Well, after all, you're the chief's son."

"And one day I'll be chief. Then you'll have to do everything I say."

"What will you tell me to do?"

"Maybe I'll make you go out and keep chickens for me or something like that."

Laski joined them as they walked on. Dixie had never met anybody she was more fond of than Wamba and his sister. The three of them had become inseparable.

"Where are you going?" Laski asked.

"Going to show Dixie the new animals."

They came to a pen where sheep were kept.

Dixie looked in and cried, "Oh, look! Baby sheep! They're brand-new!"

"Just born last night. I knew you liked all baby animals," Wamba said. "You want to hold one?"

"Yes!"

They went inside the small corral, and Dixie ran to a lamb that was staggering around, barely able to walk. She picked him up. Then she sat down with him, crooning and stroking his wool. "Oh, he's so cute!"

"Yes, I think he'll be delicious." Wamba said this with a straight face. Of course, he knew that would irritate Dixie—which it did.

"How can you say such a thing!"

"Well, he *will* be delicious! That's what lambs are for—to eat. What did you think? That we would lead him around on a leash like you do Flash?"

"I don't want to talk about it!"

"You never want to talk about anything unpleasant. But I can't see that eating lamb is unpleasant. You eat lamb at your house, don't you?"

"But I don't talk about it," Dixie said primly. She ignored Wamba then, and she and Laski played with the three baby lambs. One of them was coal black.

"This one will be a real Masai warrior," Laski said. "See how pretty he is? And he's as black as night."

Wamba leaned against a post of the corral. "You read us once about the old days of the Bible when they killed little lambs," he said thoughtfully.

Dixie had read the Passover story from the book of Exodus. She had not thought Wamba had been listening but evidently he had. "Yes," she said. "That was what God's people did."

"How did they do it?" Wamba asked with interest.

"Oh, I don't know!"

"I bet they cut their throats," Wamba said.

Dixie knew he did not have her love for small animals. To him they were useful for giving milk and to eat. One had to own animals—that was the way the Masai lived —but they did not get attached to them in the same way that she did.

"Why did they do that?" he asked curiously.

Dixie was holding the black lamb now and stroking its fleece. The lamb reached up and licked her chin. "Well, you see, the world was spoiled by Adam and Eve. You remember that story?"

"Yes. I remember it."

"Well, someone had to die for the sins of the people."

"Each man could die for his own sin," Wamba said thoughtfully. "That would be fair."

"But then we would all have to die and be forever shut away from God. No," Dixie said, "the Bible says that the lamb was just a sort of picture of what was going to happen."

"How do you mean—what was going to happen?" Wamba asked with interest. He stood on one foot as the Masai men did. To Dixie it was a wonder that they could perch on one leg like big cranes or flamingos.

"Well, it's like this," she said. "One day God sent a man to preach. And when he saw Jesus, he said, 'Behold, the Lamb of God who takes away the sin of the world!'"

"But Jesus wasn't a lamb."

Dixie struggled to give the right explanation. It was very difficult. She had learned all of this in Sunday school when she was barely able to talk. But Laski and Wamba asked hard questions.

"Well," she said again, "it's like this. Every time the Jewish people would take a little lamb and kill it, it was God's way of teaching them that one day He would provide a *real* sacrifice. Not a lamb but a man—His Son Jesus.

"So when that preacher said, 'Here's the Lamb of God,' he was saying, 'This is the Man that you've been looking at in a sort of picture.' The lambs were *just* pictures. Their blood couldn't take away sin. But Jesus' blood could. He was saying that Jesus would be killed as a sacrifice, and when He was, all the sins of the world would be paid for. You know that part."

*"What is all this talk?"*

Startled, Dixie looked up to see Chief Tombono staring at the three of them over the top rail of the sheep pen.

"I was just telling—"

"I know! You were telling them about Jesus God. I do not want you to teach my son. He is Masai. He will be a warrior. And then he will be an elder. And then he will be chief. The old ways will be his ways."

"But, Chief—"

"No more! You hear? No more talk of Jesus God!"

Dixie swallowed hard as the chief glared at her, then turned and walked away. "He saved my life from that crocodile," she said, "but he doesn't like me."

"He likes you fine, Dixie," Laski said. "He just doesn't like Jesus."

"He likes the old ways. That's all he knows," Wamba said sadly.

That noon, when Dixie ate with her parents, she told them what had happened. Then she asked, "Dad, what shall I do? He told me not to talk to them about Jesus anymore."

"There's not much you can do, Dixie," her father said. A sad look came into his eyes. "All these people know is spirit worship and myths. We can't just come rushing in and proclaim the gospel and expect that they'll understand it the first time. After all," he added, "even back home in the States, some people hear the gospel for years and refuse to believe it."

"But what do I do, Dad?"

"Be kind, be gentle, always show respect to Chief Tombono, and you must obey what he says."

"But he lets them come to Sunday school!"

"I'm thankful for that," her mother put in. "And you can talk to them all you want in Sunday school. For some reason, he doesn't mind that. I think he wants them to learn English. But when he sees you three becoming such fast friends, he's afraid that you will lead his son into the new ways."

"The people are all terrified of the witch doctor," Dixie said thoughtfully. "Do you think he can really make people die?"

"I think fear can do all kinds of things. They *think* he can make them die. And when a person lives under fear like that, strange things can happen to him. No, I don't believe all the things that Maugombo tells them, but they do. And at the same time, Satan is strong."

"All right. I'll be very careful, but I'll pray every day that Chief Tombono will be saved."

"We'll all agree on that. Let's pray for him right now."

It was only thirty minutes later that Wamba came to the door. "Trader come," he announced.

"I hate to see that," Mr. Morris said.

"What's wrong, Dad?" Dixie wanted to know.

"It's that Miller. He comes here and literally robs the people. He gives them pennies for the things they work so hard for—skins of animals, plumage of birds, even pearls that they find in the mussels in the river. I wish he'd never come here!"

When Dixie was on the way to see what was happening, she said to Wamba, "My father doesn't like this man Miller."

"I don't either. I think he's a bad man."

"Does your father like him?"

"It's hard to say. He lets him come to the village, anyway."

When they got to the center of the village, Dixie saw a very tall white man with light hair and a cold face. He had come in a big truck, and it was loaded with all kinds of things he had probably collected from the people in various villages.

The trader looked at Dixie and said, "What's this?"

"Preacher's daughter," someone informed him.

Miller looked at her and smiled, but the smile did not touch his eyes. "Well, girlie, how are you today?"

"Fine, thank you," Dixie said. She stood watching as Miller bargained with the village people. Even she knew that he was cheating them. One man brought a beautiful leopard skin and traded it for just a few beads.

"Why, that skin's worth much more than that!" Dixie cried indignantly.

The man scowled. "You keep out of this, missy! This is none of your business!"

"It's my business if you don't pay them enough for what they sell you! Why, that skin would be worth many times that!" She asked Wamba to interpret for her, then said to the man who had brought the leopard skin, "You could probably get five hundred beads for that one skin!"

The Masai warrior stared at her, then at the trader.

Miller said in Swahili, "Don't pay any attention to her! She doesn't know what she's talking about."

"I do too know what I'm talking about! You ask my dad," Dixie said to the warrior. "He'll tell you."

At that moment Dixie's father arrived and put his hand on Dixie's shoulder. He said quietly, "Dixie, be quiet." She looked up at his face, and he was shaking his head.

Leading her away, he said, "Let me handle this, Dixie. What you said was right, but these people have to learn slowly, as I've told you. I've been talking to the chief about this trader, and he's begun to listen to me. Sooner or later I'll convince him that Miller is a bad thing for his people. Just give me time. I'm going to take the chief into town with me and show him how much he can get for some of these things. But not right now."

"All right, Dad. Whatever you say."

Later in the afternoon Dixie took a long walk with Flash. She returned to see that Miller was ready to leave. She would not have spoken to him, but he called out, "Hey, girlie, just a minute!"

Dixie turned and asked coldly, "What do you want, Mr. Miller?"

He came toward her, his eyes fixed on Flash. "That's a fine cheetah you got there. Where'd you get him?"

"He's mine. I traded for him."

"I bet you got him for almost nothing."

"He was starving, and I gave an expensive necklace for him!"

"Well, I'll tell you what. I'll give you a hundred dollars for him."

Dixie looked at him with astonishment. She knew what wild animals cost. She knew that the circus had paid ten thousand dollars for a single tiger. "If I wanted to sell him—which I don't—I could get a lot more than that for him, Mr. Miller."

The trader started to argue. When Dixie began to walk away, he said, "Don't walk away from me while I'm talking to you, kid!"

But Dixie went right on. She heard him say something under his breath. When she looked back, he was watching her angrily.

She told her father and mother what had happened, and Mr. Morris said, "Just stay away from him. He's no good."

Later that evening, when Dixie was sitting beside Flash, feeding him his supper, she said, "That man thought I'd sell you for a hundred dollars. Why, I wouldn't take a thousand dollars for you. Did you know that, Flash?"

Flash swallowed a big mouthful of meat. Then, seeing there was no more, he yawned, put his head down, and closed his eyes.

Dixie giggled. "You have terrible manners, Flash! You eat and go right to sleep." She stroked his head. "Don't worry. I wouldn't sell you for any price."

## 8
## PRAYER FOR A QUEEN

"What's the matter, Wamba? You look sad today."

Dixie and Wamba were fishing in the river. She'd noticed that he had said practically nothing all morning. That was unusual for him. He usually talked all the time. And now she saw a worried look in his dark brown eyes.

"It's my mother," he said.

"What's wrong with her?"

"She's very sick."

Dixie laid down her fishing pole and turned to face her friend. "I didn't know that, Wamba. When did she get sick?" she asked quietly.

"Two days ago. And she's getting worse."

"I'm so sorry. I hope she'll be better soon."

"She may die."

Dixie blinked with surprise. "What makes you say that?"

"It is a bad sickness. Last year, many of our people died of it."

"What is it?"

But Wamba did not know what the sickness was, any more than the rest of his people did.

"Do you think it would be all right if I would go visit her?"

"I—I suppose so."

They had caught little, for the fish weren't biting. They gathered up their fishing lines and left the river. And Dixie went home with Wamba.

She stooped down to enter the royal hut. A small cooking fire was burning, and it threw flickering shadows over the interior. A load of wood was stacked at one end of the house. That reminded Dixie briefly of how upset she had been when she had first seen a Masai mother carrying an enormous load of wood on her back. She discovered that men never helped with the firewood. That was women's work.

Forgetting the firewood, she turned toward Wamba's mother, who was lying on one of the two beds. She went to her side and said quietly, "Hello, Queen Minna. I'm sorry you're sick."

When the queen turned toward her, Dixie saw that she was ill indeed. She whispered something in Swahili, but Dixie could not understand it.

"She asked you to pray to your God for her," Wamba said.

"But your father might not like that."

Wamba looked disappointed but said no more. Dixie knew she had to do something. She had not said a word about Jesus to either Wamba or Laski since the chief's warning, but this seemed to be different. *Surely he wouldn't mind,* she thought, *if I just said a prayer for her.* She started to say a simple prayer.

She had not quite finished when the chief entered. He seized her arm and led her outside. "Leave now! Do not come to see my family anymore!"

Dixie cast an agonized look at Wamba, who stood off to one side.

"No more Jesus God!" the chief said sternly to him. "You will not listen to this girl, you understand?"

In Masai society, children obeyed their fathers without question. Wamba nodded.

"No more talk about Jesus God."

"But, Chief, does that mean I can't even speak to them?"

"You speak, but no more praying and no more talk about Jesus God."

"I promise, Chief."

"Do you have a good word?"

Dixie knew he was asking if she would keep her promise. "Yes. I keep my promises, and I do promise you. No more talk about Jesus until you say so."

"That will never be."

Dixie watched the chief walk off. Then she said, "I'm sorry, Wamba."

"No. It's my fault. We were the ones who asked you to pray. I will tell my father."

"No. Don't do that. There's no point in it. It's over." She wanted to say more but only said, "Your mother will be all right. I'm sure she will be."

She went home and found her father in his study. "Daddy, can I talk to you?"

"Sure, Dixie. What is it? Something wrong?" he asked. Then he listened as she explained what had happened. "Have you talked to either Wamba or Laski about Jesus since the chief warned you not to?"

"No, Dad. Not a word."

"Well, since the queen herself asked you to pray, I think it was a rather special situation. But you must not do even that again. We have to honor the chief as a father and as a leader of his people. I think he's wrong, but one day he'll see the light."

"All right, Dad. I promised him, and I'll keep my word."

Mr. Morris reached over and pulled her onto his lap. Dixie had just turned twelve, and he said, "You're getting too big to hold on my lap."

"No, I'm not." She put her arms around him. "I'll never be too big for that. Even when I'm old and fat and smother you, I'll still want to sit on your lap."

"That's my girl." He hugged her. "I'm very proud of you, Dixie. I know this is hard, but God's going to see us through. Now, let's pray for Minna to get well and for Chief Tombono to come to know Jesus."

# 9

# TROUBLE AT MIDNIGHT

**D**ixie's cork sat on the still water, seemingly frozen in place. The small lake where she and her father had come to fish early this morning was a blue gem under a light blue sky. White fleecy clouds drifted overhead, and from far off came the cry of a bird that sounded like someone yodeling. "Dad, what kind of bird is that?"

A smile creased Mr. Morris's face. "I'm afraid I don't know, Dixie. It would take a lifetime to learn the names of half the birds and animals in this part of the world."

"I've learned a lot of them already," she said. "And I've learned the Swahili names for some of them, too."

"You've done a fine job of making a difficult adjustment. A great many people who come out from the comforts of home in the

States just can't make it around here," he said. "You wouldn't believe how many people come out to visit the mission fields and can't even last two weeks. Of course, some of them get sick and have to go home. They can't help that. But it's hard on most North Americans coming here, and it takes a while to get used to doing without things. But you've done fine, Dixie."

They fished without speaking for a while. Dixie felt good. She had missed her father and mother greatly during the time that she had been alone in the States. Now occasionally she would turn just to look at him. He sat with his eyes half closed against the bright glow of the rising sun on the lake. She found herself breathing a little prayer, thanking God for bringing her to be with her parents.

That had become a habit of hers lately. In the silence of the night and the long, slow days that seemed to move by effortlessly, she had begun to offer up prayers of thanks to God for the little things that she had always taken for granted. Even a glass of cool water was something to be thankful for now.

Suddenly her dad said, "Your mother

and I need to make a long trip tomorrow over to the village by the big river. I think you wouldn't enjoy that much."

"Oh, I can stay here by myself."

"I wouldn't ask you to do that. But Nanine will stay with you, if you wouldn't be afraid."

Indignant, Dixie began to pout. "Afraid! Dad, you know I'm not afraid."

"Well, you'll be all right, I'm sure. But it'll be just you and Nanine alone in the house. We'll probably not get back till the next morning."

"I'll be fine. I'll go inside early, and I'll listen to the radio and work on the crossword puzzle."

"Well, if you're sure." He grinned at her suddenly. "You're getting to be a big girl —really a young lady. Twelve years old now."

Dixie always felt good when her father said things like that. There were times when she wanted to grow up quickly and could not wait until she was sixteen. But at other times she still liked to be babied occasionally by her parents, especially her father.

Suddenly there was a loud *plop!*

Dixie's eyes shot back to where her cork had been. It was not there. There was only a widening circle. Her line began to dash through the water, and she leaped to her feet, crying, "I got one!" She hauled back on the line and discovered that she could not pull it in. "It must be a whale, Daddy!" she cried.

"Hang on! Don't give him any slack!"

"I won't! I won't!"

The fish took off down along the bank, and it took all her strength to hold him back. She stepped out into the mud, braced her back, and then slowly began to pull the fish in.

Her father kept calling encouragement, and when the fish came close to the bank, he reached down quickly, grabbed it by the gills, and heaved it onto the shore.

"What a monster!" he said.

"Oh, what kind is it?" Dixie cried. She came close to look at the huge fish. It was more than a foot and a half long. "It's the biggest fish I ever caught!"

"I don't know what it is, but I'll bet it's good to eat. Just what I needed—fresh fish for supper. Well, no sense staying any longer. We've got enough fish for us and to give some to Wamba and Laski too. Maybe we'll invite them over to supper tonight."

"Oh, that'll be great, Dad!" Dixie looked

at her fish with admiration. "Back home I'll bet I'd never catch a fish this big."

"I guess you wouldn't. Well, let's get back to the house. Cleaning this thing is going to be a job."

The supper proved to be magnificent, Dixie thought. Laski and Wamba sat shyly at the table. They had never eaten with the Morrises before, and both acted bashful. It seemed strange to them to eat from plates. Dixie, however, tried to make them feel at home, and they seemed to enjoy the meal. Afterward, everyone listened to the radio, and that delighted the two Masai youngsters.

The next morning, Dixie got up before dawn and cooked breakfast while her parents prepared to leave. As they pulled away in the Land Rover, her mother called back, "Be sure you don't wander off. And be sure to lock yourself in tonight, Dixie!"

"I will, Mom. You two have a good time. I'll take care of everything here."

Dixie quickly performed her chores. She cleaned the house, washed the dishes, and made the beds. Then she went out to spend some time with Flash. It was a beautiful day with a clear sky.

She and the cheetah went down to where Wamba was taking his family's cattle out to another pen. She walked along with him, and he began to point out the fine points of the huge animals. The cows walked slowly, their heads bobbing. Many of them had huge markings on their sides. One marking was a circle with something that looked like a star in the middle. Rays radiated from it.

"That's our family's mark. Everybody knows it. If one of our cattle strays away, someone will bring it back."

"Are there any cattle rustlers here?"

Wamba looked puzzled. "What is that?" And he listened to Dixie explain about the men who stole cows back in the early American West. Then he nodded. "Oh yes, the Masai are great cattle thieves." He seemed very proud of this.

Dixie said, "Don't you think that's wrong?"

"Wrong to do what?"

"Why, to steal cattle."

But Wamba could see nothing wrong with it. For years the Masai had gone on cattle raids. It was part of their culture. They did not look on it as particularly wrong, but much less cattle stealing went on now than in the old days.

They spent the morning together. Then Dixie made peanut butter sandwiches for both Wamba and his sister. They had never eaten peanut butter before—or even seen a sandwich!

"It sticks to your mouth," Laski complained.

"It does, but it's good," Dixie said. The peanut butter had to be hauled out from the city and was hard to find, but she was glad to share it with her friends.

Then the three of them went for another walk around the village.

Wamba said suddenly, "Look. That trader, Miller, is back again."

And then Dixie saw the man's large truck, piled high with goods. "I don't even want to see him. He's not a good man," she said.

Laski, however, wanted to see what he had. "He always has pretty things. Let's go look. Maybe my father will buy me something."

As soon as they walked up to the truck, Miller fixed his eyes on Dixie. He smiled, but as before the smile did not go to his eyes. They were cold and hard. "Well, if it isn't the missionary girl. How are you today, missy?"

"Very nice," Dixie said politely.

"You still got that cheetah cub?"

"Yes sir, I do."

"Well," Miller said, "I've got a buyer for him. I'll give you two hundred dollars for him. Cold cash. Think of what a girl could buy with that much money."

"No, I don't want to sell him, Mr. Miller."

Again, he tried to persuade her. It was easy to see that the man was used to having his own way and that he was getting angry. Finally Dixie just turned and walked away so that she would not have to listen to him.

"She's a stuck-up one," Miller said to Maugombo. The two were speaking in whispers.

The trader and the witch doctor were often seen together, and Dixie's father had once said, "I think that witch doctor is somehow in business with Miller. He encourages the people to practically give their things to him for a few cheap beads in return."

Maugombo grinned evilly. "You want cheetah?"

"Yes. I can get a lot of money for him, but she won't sell him."

A sly look crossed the face of the witch doctor. His eyes were cold and penetrating. When he grinned, his teeth were yellow. Many were missing. "I can get him for you."

"How?"

"The girl is alone. Tonight she will lock herself in and go to sleep. It will be easy for me to get the animal. What will you give me?"

"Fifty dollars."

"You offered the girl two hundred!"

Miller chuckled. "A hundred then. That's more money than you've ever seen in your life, Maugombo. You can buy whatever you want with that much hard money."

Finally Maugombo nodded. "All right. I will do it. I will have the cheetah for you at midnight—five hours after the sun goes down. The girl must be asleep before I take him."

"The cat might put up a fight," Miller suggested.

"No, she has made him into a pet. And

she keeps him in a pen that is not locked. I will take some meat."

"I still don't know if the cheetah will leave. You'd better put him in some kind of a cage."

"I will take care of that. You have the money ready for me."

"At midnight, then. I'll wait for you. As soon as I get the cat, I'll be gone. Be careful you don't get caught. The missionary could make trouble for us both."


Dixie locked the doors before sundown.

Nanine, the elderly Masai woman who sometimes helped with the cooking and cleaning had come to spend the night. Dixie made a bed for her on the floor of the main room and talked with her for awhile. But the old woman soon grew sleepy and lay down. She closed her eyes and went to sleep almost at once.

Dixie did not feel like sleeping, and she stayed up until after ten listening to the shortwave radio. Somehow she found a Christian station that was playing some of the songs she had learned to love back in the States. She listened until she finally grew sleepy. She wrote a short letter to her uncle and aunt, then read a chapter in the Bible and got ready for bed.

She was tired but not at all afraid, as her father had suggested she might be. She got into bed, said a prayer for her parents and for Chief Tombono, as she always did, then dropped off into a dreamless sleep.

Wamba could not go to sleep. He was worrying about the cattle. There had been talk of hyenas moving into the village area. At last he got up. Everyone else was asleep, including his parents. His mother was still sick, though not as sick as she had been. He knew that Dixie was praying for her.

Leaving the house, Wamba started toward the pens where the cattle were kept at the edge of the village. His sharp ears picked up the sound of their lowing, and farther out he heard the cry of wild dogs. The wild dogs alone would not bring down a cow, but hyenas in a pack could. He knew they were far more apt to get to the cattle than a lion or a leopard was.

Overhead the stars were twinkling. He looked up, wondering briefly how many there were. He was passing the house of the witch doctor, Maugombo, when a strange sound caught his attention. He stood still, not moving. It was a creaking sound.

Wamba crept forward silently. He had learned how to stalk birds and game, and his feet made no sound. He barely allowed himself to breathe.

And then the bright moonlight revealed Maugombo and another man, a tall bulky figure. Wamba recognized Maugombo's servant. The man had little judgment, but he was very strong, and he was pulling what appeared to be a cart. When Wamba moved closer still, he saw that, indeed, it was a two-wheeled cart. On it was a sort of cage.

Curiosity filled Wamba. *I wonder what the witch doctor is doing. He is up to no good, I'll bet.*

Wamba was afraid of Maugombo. He had heard the bad stories that were told about him. But as the two men walked along, the stronger one pulling the cart, he made a decision. *I'm going to follow them and see what they're up to.*

Wamba kept to the side of the road, darting behind trees. He stayed back just far enough so that he could see them but was sure that they could not see him.

And then they stopped—in front of the missionary's house!

Wamba moved closer yet. *What are they doing at Dixie's house?* he wondered. *Her parents are not home.* Then fear came over him. *Maybe they're going to kidnap her and sell her as a slave!*

That did not seem likely, but it helped Wamba resolve to get as close as possible. He crept forward. And he saw Maugombo open the cheetah's pen.

*They're taking Flash!*

When the cheetah came to him, the witch doctor spoke to him quietly and gave him something. He seemed to be feeding the animal. Then Flash, who was very tame, followed Maugombo to the cart. The witch doctor threw more meat into the open cage, and Flash leaped in to get it. At once Maugombo slammed the door and fastened it.

"Now I have you! Let's get out of here."

Wamba did not know what to do. He followed the creaking cart for a few hundred yards. Then he stood still and found himself whispering, "Jesus God, help me to know what to do." He stood for a moment longer. Then he turned and ran back toward Dixie's house.

## 10

## CAPTURED

**D**ixie heard scratching, but she was so sound asleep that it did not awaken her completely. She lay there in that state that is not quite being asleep and yet is not quite being awake. The sound came again. She thought, *It's probably that goat bumping against the house again.*

But she failed to go back to sleep, and the scratching continued. And then Dixie stiffened, for she heard her name being called in a low but insistent voice.

Coming off the bed in one motion, Dixie ran to the window. She looked down through the bars. "Wamba, what are you doing here?"

"There is trouble, Dixie."

"Is it about my parents?"

"No." In the moonlight she could see

him shake his head. He looked fearfully toward the road. "It is Maugombo."

"Maugombo! What's he done?"

"He has taken Flash. Stolen him."

Dixie stood frozen at the window, not able to understand. "Tell me what happened."

Wamba told how he had left his house to look to the safety of the cattle and had seen Maugombo. He ended the story by saying, "And so they have Flash in a cage, and they are taking him away somewhere."

"Let me get dressed," Dixie said. "We've got to do something." Quickly she closed the shutters and dressed as fast as possible. She tiptoed by Nanine and saw that she was still asleep. She let herself out, and the bright moonlight fell on Wamba as he came toward her. "Maugombo must be in with that trader," Dixie said. "That's the only reason he would want Flash."

"I think so," Wamba agreed. "He was there when Miller offered you money for the cheetah. What are we going to do? Shall I get my father?"

"No," Dixie said quickly. "Not yet." She wished desperately that her own father were there. "Daddy's gone and won't be back until tomorrow," she said thoughtfully.

"By that time they will be far, far away."

Dixie knew that once Flash was taken off in Miller's big truck, it would be hopeless. There would be no way to catch up with him. Fear gripped her, for she had come to love the cheetah. "I've got to follow them. Will you go with me, Wamba?"

Wamba hesitated. "It is dangerous in the jungle at night. There are leopards and hyenas."

"God can take care of us. He won't let anything happen." Dixie looked at Wamba and waited.

The boy was a Masai, and she knew the Masai valued courage above all other virtues. One day he would be a warrior, and already he was looking forward to that day. Here was a chance to prove his courage.

Wamba straightened up and said proudly, "I'm not afraid. Come. We will get Flash back."

"Good. But first let's pray. We need God's care."

"It is good to pray. My mother is getting well—because you prayed for her, I think."

"And you've been praying, Wamba." Dixie bowed her head and noticed that

Wamba did, also. She said, "Lord, You know everything about us. Help us to get Flash back. Keep us safe from wild animals. Let nothing happen to us. Thank You for Wamba, who is such a good friend as to go into danger with me because we are friends. Help us now. In the name of Jesus."

Wamba said, "The cart will not be hard to follow."

Indeed the thieves were not hard to follow. The moonlight was bright. The wheels of the cart had cut into the trail. And Wamba had sharp eyes. He was accustomed to tracking cattle who were lost.

"Stay behind me," he whispered. His eyes kept looking from side to side, alert always. He seemed to be listening for the sound of anything that might be dangerous.

As they hurried down the road, Dixie tried not to be afraid. She could not imagine what it would be like to be attacked by a leopard or by a pack of the wild dogs that roved the country. She continued to pray, and she kept close behind Wamba.

She did not know how far they had gone, but now the foliage grew thicker and they passed into a heavily wooded area.

They were on a wider road now—the main one from the city.

Wamba said, "Here are the tracks of your parents' car. And these are from the big truck of Miller."

"But can you see the cart tracks?"

"Yes. They are the freshest of all. We must be quiet now. We may be getting close."

"What will we do?" Dixie said.

"We will sneak up and hide ourselves. When we get a chance we will take Flash and run. But we must be careful. I think Miller is a dangerous man. Perhaps more dangerous than hyenas."

They pressed on through the moonlit darkness until at last Wamba whispered, "There. There they are up ahead."

And then Dixie saw Miller's big truck standing by the roadside. As they moved closer as quietly as possible, she could hear two voices.

Wamba put a finger to his lips, then whispered in her ear. "There is the cart. If they leave it alone, I will open the door, and then we must run."

"All right," Dixie whispered back.

The night was still bright. Taking care

not to be seen, they crept close enough so that two figures were plainly visible. Dixie recognized Miller at once. He towered over the wizened witch doctor. Over to one side stood the huge servant of Maugombo, saying nothing.

"So you got him," she heard Miller say. He laughed aloud. "I didn't think you could do it."

"You do not know me, Miller," the witch doctor said. "I can do anything with these people."

"Well, it's a lucky day for me—and for you too."

"Give me the money."

Dixie watched Miller reach into his pocket and pull out some paper money.

"No! Hard money!" Maugombo said.

"I don't have that much hard money on me. This paper money is just as good."

"No! Hard money!" the witch doctor insisted.

They argued back and forth.

Finally Maugombo said to the servant in Swahili, "Go back to the house."

The servant plodded away, and Dixie and Wamba listened to Miller and Maugombo argue on.

At last Miller agreed to give Maugombo the goods that he wanted, instead of hard money. Dixie guessed that the witch doctor himself was being cheated, for Miller was crafty.

And then the trader brought out a bottle, saying, "We'll have a drink on it."

The men began to drink together.

Dixie and Wamba were hiding behind the same tree, looking out from opposite sides. "Maybe they will drink so much they will fall asleep. Then it will be easy," Wamba whispered.

Dixie hoped so. She was thinking again, *If he drives off with Flash in the truck, there's no way to catch him.*

Suddenly something strong gripped her arm. At the same time, Wamba cried out. Looking around, Dixie saw the huge servant of Maugombo grinning down at them.

The man let out a loud cry.

"Who's that?" Miller shouted and put his hand on the gun that he always carried at his side.

"Wait! It is my servant!" Maugombo said. He peered into the shadows. Then he laughed aloud. "And see what we have caught."

Miller laughed, too, when he saw Dixie and Wamba, both in the grip of the big servant. "Well, we got ourselves more than a cheetah. We got a missionary kid and the chief's son."

"You'd better let us go! And I want my cheetah back!" Dixie cried.

Miller laughed again. "Well, you've got nerve, missy. I'll say that for you."

"My father will not permit you to steal the cheetah," Wamba said. "Let us take the cheetah and go, and we will say nothing."

"Not so fast," Miller said. "What makes you think I'd trust you?"

Then Maugombo said, "We have more here than you think, Miller."

"What do you mean by that, witch doctor?"

"I mean this is the *chief's* son, his only son. He will give anything he has for him, and he has much wealth. He will give all he possesses to get this son back alive."

"Oh, a kidnapping and a ransom! Is that what you mean?"

"I do not know those words," Maugombo snorted, "but if you send word that he is being held and will die if Tombono's treasures are not given, he will give them."

Miller's rough face was filled with thought.

Dixie protested, "That's against the law even in Africa! You know what they do to people that kidnap others."

"You shut up!" Miller said. Greed showed itself plainly in his eyes. He said, "All right. Maugombo, you go back and tell the chief that his son has been captured. Tell him he was kidnapped not by me but by some roving white men."

"You write a message. It will say all this."

"I'll do that, and you take it to him. I'll tell him to send the treasure by you to this place. No one else must come."

Miller went to the truck and reappeared shortly with a sheet of paper in his hand.

"What about these two?" Maugombo asked.

"I'll take care of them." He handed the paper to the witch doctor and then went back to the truck. He was gone for a few moments, then returned with some chains. "We'll wait right here," he said.

Taking Dixie's arm, Miller locked cuffs about her wrists and chained her to a tree.

He did the same thing with Wamba. "They won't go anywhere now."

"What you say on this paper?"

"I told him that if he doesn't send what I ask for, I'll send his son's head back to him in a basket."

Maugombo grinned. "He will send it. Never fear. You wait here." Motioning to his servant to follow, he disappeared into the shadows.

As soon as the witch doctor was gone, Miller turned back to his two captives. "Bad luck, youngsters, but that's the way it goes!" He added, "But don't worry. I'll let you go as soon as I get what I want."

Dixie and Wamba both sat down at the base of the tree. They did not say a word, but Dixie began to silently pray. *Lord, why did You let this happen?* But she knew she had to keep on trusting God, so she said, *Even now, Lord, I know You can get us out of this.*

She reached over and took Wamba's hand. "We'll just keep on praying, Wamba," she whispered. "Jesus won't let us down."

The fierce light of the Masai people shown in Wamba's eyes. "I am not afraid. I believe in Jesus God."

## 11
# THE TEST

**M**augombo had been in a position of great power in the village for many years. He was not a good man. He had little kindness and was filled with selfishness. He was also a crafty man. He spent much time planning exactly what to do to rob Chief Tombono of his riches. He had long been envious of the chief, and now was his chance to lay his hands on what he wanted.

Back in the village, Maugombo did not go at once to the chief. It was his habit to think long and hard about any serious step. He well knew that Tombono could be a hard man, and he sat for a long time in his house before a flickering fire, just thinking. His face was frozen, but his eyes were alive as he thought of many plans and discarded them.

"If Miller's plan works," he muttered to himself, "Chief Tombono will give up his wealth. But the boy, Wamba—he will tell him that *I* was involved. That will not do." A shiver ran over him as he thought of the powerful Masai chief. With his own eyes he had seen Tombono kill a lion single-handedly with a spear. Though Maugombo had much influence with the chief, he knew that, where the boy was concerned, there would be no mercy.

"I will get the boy alone and put a terrible curse on him," he decided. "I will tell him that, if he breathes one word of this, he will die the most awful death. And his family will all die, also." He nodded then, and a smile turned the corners of his thin lips upward. "He is only a boy. He will be afraid to tell."

Then he continued to sit in front of the fire, trying to find a way to cheat Miller. "I must be careful," he muttered, "or he will get more than I. But he is not as smart as I am. I will arrange to bring what he calls the ransom money, but all of it will not reach Miller. I will hide most of it, and then we will divide what I do take to him. He will never know." He chuckled and nodded and muttered into the fire until dawn came.

* * *

Maugombo went early to the house of the chief and cried out, "Chief Tombono! Chief Tombono! An evil has come!"

Almost at once Tombono came out of his house. "What is it, Maugombo?" he demanded. "What's wrong?"

"An evil thing has come. I was walking early this morning, just before dawn, when a messenger brought this. A white man."

"Miller?"

"No. Not Miller. Miller is gone. The strange man gave me this."

Tombono took the piece of paper and frowned. "This is white man's writing. I cannot read it."

"I cannot read it, either, but I know it is something bad. He said it is about your son, Wamba."

Shock raced across the chief's face. He said harshly and quickly, "What about my son?"

"He has been captured by the white men. Some were through here, you remember, six moons ago. Not Miller. Two others."

"I remember them. I ran them out of the village."

"Yes. They must have formed a hatred for you, O Chief, and now they get back at you through your son."

"What do they want?"

Maugombo shook his head. "I do not know. The man told me to bring this paper to you."

"The Jesus man can read this."

"Ah, yes, but he left the village yesterday and will not be back for a time."

"How do you know this?"

"I heard the white girl say so to your son."

"Then I will call a meeting of the elders. We must decide what to do."

"You must be very careful. These are evil men. They will harm your son."

"If I can get to them, they will harm no one!"

"Ah, but we do not know where they are. We must be wise, O Chief. Wait and let the white man read what the paper says."

Tombono nodded reluctantly. "Very well. We will wait."

Mr. Morris was tired as he and his wife drove down the winding road toward home. He was glad to reach the narrow trail that had been hacked out by axes to allow his vehicle to get in and out of the village. It also was used by a few traders such as Miller.

"I'm so tired I can hardly move," Mrs. Morris said, stretching. "And you didn't sleep at all last night, did you?"

"About an hour. I'm pretty tired, too." He looked at his watch. "It's almost ten o'clock. I figured we'd be back before now."

"You're not worried about Dixie, are you?"

"Oh, no. She'll be all right. She promised she'd lock herself in, and you know how she is about keeping her word."

The Land Rover kept lurching along over the rough road. They could go no more than four or five miles an hour over some of it and no more than fifteen over the *good* parts.

Finally he said, "Well, there's the village. I'll be glad to get home."

Then Mrs. Morris looked in the direction of their house. She sat up straight. "Look! There's a crowd around our house! Something must have happened to Dixie. I just know something has!"

"Now, don't get excited. Maybe the people just want to have a meeting." Dixie's father was troubled himself, but he did not want his wife to be more alarmed. He wished suddenly that they had not left Dixie alone, but he did not say so. He stopped the Land Rover in front of the house and got out, noting that Chief Tombono and the elders were there, as well as Maugombo.

"What's wrong, Chief?" he asked.

Tombono held up a piece of paper. "Evil white men have my son. They write on paper. You read."

"Where is Dixie?" Mrs. Morris asked Tombono.

"Not here. I do not know."

Dixie's father took the note. He read it, then read it aloud in Swahili. "We have your son and the missionary girl. If you do not send us the treasures out of your treasure house, you will never see them again. Send them by the witch doctor to the big baobab tree at the main road. He must come alone."

"How did this happen?" Dixie's mother cried.

"How did the note come, Chief?" her dad asked.

"I brought it," Maugombo said. "A white man stopped me this morning and gave it to me. He told me to bring it to the chief. But we could not read it. So we wait for you."

"What do you think, Chief?"

"We must get my son back."

"And my daughter. But how can we find them?" He turned to Maugombo and demanded, "Where did you see this man?"

"Over by the anthill where the two big trees stand."

"They won't have the children there," Mr. Morris said. He put his arm around his wife, whispering, "Don't be afraid. It'll be all right."

Tombono said, "We will find them. We will follow their tracks."

"When they see you coming, they will kill your son," Maugombo warned quickly. "You must do just as they say."

From the look on the chief's face, Mr. Morris knew that he desperately wanted to have an enemy to fight. Tombono had had much trouble recently. He had been concerned for his wife, Minna. And now he was thinking of his son, who one day would be chief in his stead. He had many daughters but only one son. No doubt, the fierce blood of the Masai boiled up in him.

But the chief was surely aware that Maugombo was right, Dixie's father thought. They could bring death to both youngsters by following the witch doctor. And if he simply sent the treasure, the children could be killed anyway.

"We must be very wise, Chief," the missionary said quietly.

"Yes. We must be wise. Though I want to fight."

"I'm afraid this battle won't be fought with spears or knives. It is going to take the power of God to get our children back safely." He fought down the fear that was in him. He felt his wife tremble as she clung to him. Once again he said to her, "Don't worry. God will help us."

"You think your God can help?" Maugombo sneered.

Bill Morris looked at the witch doctor. "I always pray when I'm in trouble. And this is the most trouble I've ever been in."

"It is the worst thing that has ever happened to me too." Chief Tombono stood tall and straight as a tree. He looked at the elders gathered about him. "Come. We will talk, and then we will decide what to do."

The missionaries watched the Masai

walk away. The elders were the wise men of the tribe. Although the chief was the final authority, he would not make any big decision without letting the elders have their say.

"They'll consult for some time," Mr. Morris said. "In the meanwhile, we've got to pray for Dixie."

Laski came up to them. "And for Wamba too." She had tears in her eyes. "I am worried about my brother and about Dixie. Are they in very bad trouble?"

"I'm afraid so, Laski." Mrs. Morris put her arm around the small girl. "But we believe that God is strong enough to get them out of it."

"My father. What will he do?"

"I think, Laski, that your father can't do much. If it were a lion, he could fight with it. But he's not able to do that against these enemies. It will take the Lord God Almighty to do that."

"You mean Jesus God?"

"Yes. Jesus God."

"Then will you pray? My father does not like it, but I want to pray for my brother."

At noon Bill Morris looked out the window of his house and said, "Here come the chief and the elders. They must've made up their minds."

Quickly he and his wife went outside. "What have you decided, Chief?"

"The elders have spoken. This is beyond man. The gods must answer."

"I agree with that, but it must be the strong Jesus God."

Tombono narrowed his eyes. "You read story from your book—about the man of God who called fire down."

"Yes. That was Elijah."

"There were other men who had other gods."

"Yes. They were followers of a false god."

Tombono nodded. "The man said let both pray, and whichever god answers by fire, he is the true God."

Mr. Morris saw at once where this conversation was headed. But he did not know exactly what to say.

When he hesitated, Tombono said, "We have our spirits, but you come telling us of this Jesus God, who is stronger." He turned to Maugombo and said, "You pray to the spirits, Maugombo."

Maugombo hesitated, then said, "I will."

Tombono turned to the missionary. "You pray to Jesus God."

"I've already been doing that."

Tombono nodded. "We will see who is true God—the spirits of our people or this new God called Jesus. The one who answers, He will be the God I will serve."

Suddenly the missionary knew this crisis was for a purpose. Chief Tombono was the most influential man in Masailand. If such a man became a Christian, others would listen to the message of Jesus more readily. This terrible time was an opportunity for God to work.

"All right, Chief. I will pray that Jesus will give you back your son and give us back our daughter."

"It is not a time to pray," Maugombo protested. "None of the gods can do this."

"Jesus can," Dixie's father said confidently. He bowed his head. "O God, Maker of heaven and earth, Father of the Lord Jesus Christ, You hear every prayer. Now I pray that You show Chief Tombono Your power. Teach us what to do. Deliver Wamba and Dixie out of the danger they are in—in a way that shows You are the true God."

When he looked up, Mr. Morris saw

that Maugombo was watching him. But then the missionary's eyes went to Chief Tombono. He noticed a light of interest in the chief's eyes that he had never seen before. "Don't worry, Chief. I believe God is going to show you His strength."

"The God who answers, He is God," Chief Tombono said quietly.

# 12

# HOPE AT MIDNIGHT

**D**ixie pulled at the chain. It was too strong to break, as she well knew. She and Wamba watched Miller drink from his bottle. Finally he lumbered off to lie down on a cot.

The stars were still overhead, and the moon still shone, but Wamba said, "Soon it will be dawn."

"What will we do?" Dixie whispered.

But Wamba had no answers.

They sat whispering to one another until sunrise. Still Miller slept on in a drunken stupor. Both youngsters grew hot and thirsty.

Not until the sun was high in the sky did Miller wake up. He was in a surly mood. "Your father better come through with his treasure," he said threateningly to Wamba, "or it'll be too bad for you!"

Wamba did not answer.

Dixie said, "Could we have some water, please?"

Miller stared at her. Then he went to the truck, got out a jug, and waited while she drank thirstily. Wamba drank and handed back the container.

They thanked him, but Miller said nothing more. He left them, and Dixie soon smelled frying meat. They both watched as he ate. Dixie wasn't hungry.

When he finished, Miller put some greasy meat on two plates and set them down at their feet.

Dixie murmured, "Maybe we'd better eat something, Wamba. We don't know how long we'll be here."

"I will not touch his rotten meat," Wamba said fiercely. He had pulled at the cuffs until his wrists were raw and bleeding.

Dixie did not eat either.

They prayed together, then sat silently in the shade of the tree. She wanted to go to Flash, but her chain would not reach. She watched Miller—he was drinking. She had not seen him put food or water in the cheetah's cage, and she wanted to ask him to do that. But he did not return to them.

"He's drinking from his bottle again," Wamba whispered late in the afternoon. "Maybe if he gets drunk, we can get loose."

Finally she saw Miller throw himself down in the shade of the truck, and then he began to snore heavily.

Then Dixie whispered, "Wamba, look."

Wamba turned his head to see.

Dixie's hand was almost out of the cuff!

"Can you get them off?" he asked. The cuff was, indeed, much looser on her than it was on Wamba's wrist, for he was larger.

"Hand me that extrafatty meat on your plate."

"Are you going to eat it?"

"No." Dixie took the piece of greasy meat and began to rub her wrist. She greased both her wrist and hand and said in a very low whisper, "It's a good thing we had this."

Wamba watched as Dixie grasped the cuff and pulled hard. Her hand slipped out, and she whispered, "There!"

"Can you get the other one off?"

"I think so."

Dixie worked with the other cuff until it too was off.

"Good! Now run, Dixie! Get away!"

"No, I won't leave you!"

Wamba stared at her. "You must. Miller is an evil man. He may have it in his mind to kill us—even if the treasure comes."

"I won't leave you. God has been with us, and I have an idea. Let's pray again."

They prayed quietly, and then Dixie said, "Now, I just hope he doesn't wake up. I've got to do something."

"What are you going to do?" Wamba whispered, but Dixie was gone.

She tiptoed around the sleeping form of the trader. As she was almost even with him, he gave a loud cough and snort. Dixie paused, her heart leaping with fear. *He's going to wake up!* she thought. But he did not wake up, and when he settled back to snoring again, she went around the truck and stepped up onto the running board.

Her eyes searched frantically, and then she saw what she needed—a notepad and a pencil. She reached for them through the open window and then began to write. When she had filled a page, she put back the pad and pencil and stepped to the ground.

She went to the back of the truck then, and there was Flash at the door of his cage.

146

He was making the soft purring noise he always made when she came near.

"Flash," she said, "you've got to save us. You're our only hope."

She opened the door, and the cheetah began to nuzzle her. She took out of her pocket something she always carried—a piece of string. She was thankful she had it now, for there was nothing else to use. She tied the note to Flash's collar, then stepped back, and he leaped to the ground. Dixie whispered in his ear, "Home, Flash! Home! Quick!"

At once the cheetah bounded away. Dixie watched until he was out of sight, then she tiptoed back and sat down beside Wamba.

"Why did you turn him loose?"

"I put a note on his collar, telling where we are."

"Do you think he will go home?"

"He's never gone home from this far before, but he just has to, Wamba! He just has to!"

After a while, once again Wamba said, "You must go, Dixie. You can find your way back."

"No. I'm not leaving you." Dixie reached over and took his hand.

Wamba gazed at her. Then he said, "You have all the courage of a Masai, Dixie."

She knew that was the highest compliment that he could pay. "Thank you, Wamba."

"Are you not afraid?"

"A little bit."

"But Jesus God has gotten you loose from your bonds, and Flash is on his way. I believe He is going to save us."

"I believe it, too."

And they sat waiting to see what God would do.

## 13
# THE STRONG GOD

The sun was beginning to go down when Miller stirred.

Dixie whispered, "He's waking up."

"He will find the cheetah is gone, and he will be very angry."

Dixie had been worrying about that. She had been tempted more than once to run away. Still, she knew that she could not leave Wamba alone with this evil man. "Help will come soon. I'm sure of it."

"Jesus God will send my father and your father to help us." Wamba smiled at her but then turned to watch Miller. "He is up."

Miller, indeed, was up. He coughed harshly, then took a long drink of water. He looked over at the two youngsters sitting beneath the tree. He could not see that

Dixie's hands were free, so he merely grunted at them. Then he walked toward the back of the truck. He was looking in the direction of the village, but when he rounded the truck, he stopped abruptly.

"What's this!" He uttered a loud curse and grabbed the door of the open cage. "The cheetah's gone!" At once he came toward the tree and towered over the children. Then he reached down and grasped Dixie's arm. "So you got loose, did you?"

"Yes, I did, and I let Flash go! And you'd better turn us loose!"

Dixie saw the anger in the man's red face. He raised his hand as if he would hit her, then changed his mind. He stared at her instead, puzzled. "Why didn't you run off?"

"Because I won't leave my friend here!"

Miller glared at her. "You'll wish you had!" Then he turned on Wamba. "The next letter to your father will be a little bit different. It'll say that if I don't get the treasures, I'll cut off one of your fingers and send it to him. Then another, until you don't have any left!"

"I'm not afraid of you! Jesus is strong!" Wamba said defiantly.

"Oh, so you've become a Christian, have you? Well, let's see how Christian you are with one of your fingers cut off."

Grinning evilly, the trader pulled out a large pocketknife and opened it. He grabbed Wamba's hand.

"Don't you dare do that!" Dixie flew at Miller, beating at him with her fists.

The burly man laughed at her. Then he roughly shoved her away.

Dixie went flying across the ground and fell down. She leaped up at once and ran back at him. She bit his hand, and he cursed and threw her away more roughly than before.

"I'll take care of you too! Maybe *you* could do without a finger!"

Dixie was stunned, but she got to her feet. She saw the trader reach for Wamba's hand again.

But at that moment, a bloodcurdling scream rent the air. Dixie had never heard such a cry before, and it was not just from one throat but from many.

The sudden scream startled Miller so badly that he dropped Wamba's arm and reached for the gun in his belt. He had no time to draw it, however, for the clearing was suddenly filled with warriors dressed in war regalia and holding long, broad-headed spears. One of these was in the hand of Chief Tombono, and in an instant it was at the throat of the trader.

"Don't—don't kill me!"

Chief Tombono reversed the spear and struck Miller's head a blow with the butt of the shaft. It knocked the trader to the ground. Then Tombono held the point of the spear right over the big man's heart.

Dixie's father hurried to her side.

The chief looked at Mr. Morris and said, "It is your right to kill this man since your Jesus God led us here."

Dixie was holding onto her dad with all of her might, and his arms were tight around her. "I knew you'd come," she said.

"Flash brought the message. Are you all right?"

"Yes, but we wouldn't have been if you hadn't come just now."

Mr. Morris kept his arm around Dixie but turned to face Tombono.

The chief was offering him his spear.

"No," he said quietly. "I will not kill him."

"He might have killed your child and mine."

"But he won't do it now. And Christians value life, Chief. Even the lives of bad men."

"You think this man deserves to live?"

"God may be able to do something with him yet. He's the God that answers prayer. You'll have to admit that."

Chief Tombono did not move. He seemed to be thinking. But Tombono was an honest man. "Jesus God is strong," he said.

He went to his son then. He put his hand on the boy's head. "Were you afraid, my son?"

"Some. But, Father—Dixie got free. She could have left me, but she did not. She says I am her brother."

Tombono's eyes came to Dixie, and for the first time since she had known him, he smiled at her. "You are a brave girl. You are as brave as a Masai woman."

"That's what your son told me, Chief." Dixie smiled, too. She was getting over her fear now. She looked down at the ashen face of Miller, who was not moving.

The needle point of the spear was

against his chest again. Sweat was on his forehead, and his eyes were wild.

"He has broken the law, and the law will punish him. Don't kill him. Please, Chief."

The chief took a firmer grip on his spear and then looked down into the trader's eyes. "You stole my son! For this you should die!"

Miller began to plead for his life. His cries appeared to disgust all the warriors, who had gathered around. They would have died rather than plead like this.

But at last Chief Tombono turned to Dixie's dad. "You will take him to the white man's court?" he asked.

"Yes. And he will go to jail for this for a long time. Have your warriors tie him up, Chief. He won't be troubling you again. I promise."

"What about *him?*" Wamba said. "Maugombo. My father, Miller is no more guilty than the witch doctor."

An angry look leaped into the chief's face. He put a hand on Maugombo's thin arm. "What do you mean, my son?" Then he stood listening as Wamba told exactly what had happened. By the time Wamba was finished, Chief Tombono was glaring at a pale Maugombo. "You are a weak man, and your spirits are weak! I should kill you, but I will show mercy! Leave right now and never come back to the village!"

"What about all my possessions?"

"You have your life. Would you rather be dead or have them?"

With a frightened squeak, Maugombo, as soon as he was released, scurried away. He disappeared down the trail.

Chief Tombono said with certainty, "He is not a good man." Then he turned back to Dixie's father and eyed the missionary thoughtfully. "*You* are a good man. We will be friends."

"I would like that," Mr. Morris said. He squeezed Dixie and then said, "Now, let us get these chains off Wamba and get back to the village."

It was a triumphant procession that came back to Tombono's village. Mrs. Morris let out a glad cry as soon as she saw Dixie. She flew to her and threw her arms around her. "You're safe!"

"Yes!" Dixie said. "And we got Flash back."

"When he came in with the message on his collar and I saw your handwriting, I thanked God. I knew you were all right."

"Where's Flash now?"

"In his cage. I fed him and gave him some water. I think he went to sleep."

"That cheetah is a hero, Dixie," her father said. "He ought to have a medal. Maybe I'll have one made for him and put it on his collar."

"We might make him a Masai—if he had only two feet," Wamba said.

"He can be a four-footed Masai," Laski suggested.

"There's never been a four-footed Masai," her brother argued.

Dixie laughed at them both. "Well, you can have a medal made for him, Dad, but I think he'd rather have some pork."

"We'll get him a whole pig," her father said, "if that's what you want."

Dixie especially enjoyed church the next Sunday. Chief Tombono was there—with his whole family, for Minna was much better. The chief stood tall and straight, listening to her father preach about Jesus and how He could give a man a new heart. As Dixie watched the chief's face, suddenly she knew that something had changed.

Leaning over to Wamba, standing beside

her, she said, "I think your father is different today."

"He is different. He says he believes now in the Jesus God."

"Soon your mother will be saved and then others."

"Jesus God is strong," Wamba said.

Chief Tombono looked over to see who was talking. He frowned at first, but then he smiled broadly and nodded at Dixie.

"See. He likes you now. He always did, but now he has Jesus in his heart."

After the Sunday noon meal, Dixie let Flash out of his cage. She ran as fast as she could, and the cheetah kept a lazy pace alongside her. When they were out of sight of the village and had come to the river, she sat down, panting hard.

The cheetah sat beside her, and she put an arm around him. Then the two of them just watched the water, which was broken by the splashing of a fish from time to time. Dixie thought of how wonderful God had been to deliver them from their dangers. She hugged Flash and said, "God used *you* to save us, Flash."

The big cat licked her face and seemed

to smile. His eyes were large and intelligent, and he grumbled deep in his throat. It was as if he was saying, "It's all right. I didn't mind."

Dixie looked out over the flat land on the other side of the river. Viewing the odd-shaped trees and the antelope herd that was leaping across the plain kept her silent for a long time.

Then she hugged the cheetah again, saying, "You know, Flash, it's going to be great living in Africa."

Moody Press, a ministry of Moody Bible Institute, is designed for education, evangelization, and edification. If we may assist you in knowing more about Christ and the Christian life, please write us without obligation: Moody Press, c/o MLM, Chicago, Illinois 60610.